The
Goodbye
Cat

Berkley Titles by Hiro Arikawa and
Translated by Philip Gabriel

∽

The Travelling Cat Chronicles
The Goodbye Cat

The
Goodbye
Cat

SEVEN CAT STORIES

HIRO ARIKAWA

Translated from the Japanese
by Philip Gabriel

BERKLEY ∫ NEW YORK

BERKLEY
An imprint of Penguin Random House LLC
penguinrandomhouse.com

Copyright © 2021 by Hiro Arikawa
Translation copyright © 2023 by Philip Gabriel
First published in the United Kingdom, in 2023, by Doubleday, an imprint of Transworld.
Transworld is part of the Penguin Random House group of companies.

Originally published in Japanese as *Mitorineko* by Kodansha Ltd, Tokyo, in 2021.

Publication rights for this English edition arranged through Kodansha Ltd, Tokyo

Library of Congress Cataloging-in-Publication Data

Names: Arikawa, Hiro, 1972– author. | Gabriel, Philip, 1953– translator.
Title: The goodbye cat: seven cat stories / Hiro Arikawa; translated
from the Japanese by Philip Gabriel.
Other titles: Mitorineko. English
Description: New York: Berkley, 2023.
Identifiers: LCCN 2023025946 (print) | LCCN 2023025947 (ebook) |
ISBN 9780593815700 (hardcover) | ISBN 9780593815717 (ebook)
Subjects: LCSH: Cats—Fiction. | LCGFT: Short stories.
Classification: LCC PL867.5.R54 M5813 2023 (print) |
LCC PL867.5.R54 (ebook) | DDC 895.63/6—dc23/eng/20230623
LC record available at https://lccn.loc.gov/2023025946
LC ebook record available at https://lccn.loc.gov/2023025947

Printed in the United States of America
1st Printing

Text illustrations by Yukata Murakami
Title page art: cat illustration © Rita Ko / Shutterstock.com
Book design by Laura K. Corless

The Goodbye Cat

A small dish of soy sauce sat on the dining table. A couple of grains of rice floated in it, left over from breakfast, no doubt. The dining table was covered by a light blue tablecloth printed with a random pattern of small flowers.

Kota Sakuraba placed a palm into the soy sauce, then pushed it firmly onto the tablecloth, being careful to avoid the flowers. He left his palm there for a bit, then lifted it to reveal a small, soy sauce–colored plum blossom print.

Not bad, not bad at all.

Gazing at his work, Kota again dipped his palm in the soy sauce. Then again, and again. More and more soy sauce–colored plum flowers bloomed on the blue cloth.

I'm in the zone today.

He was about to make a fifth and a sixth print when—

"Hiromi! Stop that!" Mom scolded.

Damn, I'm busted, thought Kota, ears pinned back against his head.

And then—

"Did I do something?"

It was Hiromi, in the hallway, peeking uncertainly into the living room. He was the Sakuraba family's second son.

Kota was the Sakurabas' third-eldest son—scratch that, *cat*—but Kota considered himself the second eldest, with Hiromi as the third in line.

"Goodness," Mom said, seeing Hiromi in the doorway. She burst out laughing. "Sorry! I'm wrong. It's Kota. He's being an artist again."

That's what the Sakuraba family called it when Kota made his little paw prints: he was *being an artist*.

Kota found this hard to fathom, since it wasn't like he was painting a picture.

"You're at it again, eh?" Hiromi said, coming over and giving Kota a gentle flick of the finger on his forehead.

"Please don't do that, *Kota*," Mom said. "Our tablecloths have your paw prints all over them." She grabbed Kota under his belly, and wiped his soy-soaked paw vigorously with a damp dishcloth. Kota didn't like feeling wet, and so he quickly withdrew his paw and began to lick it.

"Hey, Mom, I wanted to say the same thing to you: *please don't do that*. I don't like these false accusations."

"Ah, sorry. It just came out. I never make that mistake with Masahiro."

The mistake Mom always made was to mix up Hiromi's and Kota's names. She never called Masahiro, who was Hiromi's elder brother, *Kota* by mistake. All three shared the same Chinese character in their written names, though in Kota's case, it was pronounced differently.

"Well, it seems like it's the youngest child's fate to be confused with the family cat."

"Really?" asked Mom.

"I looked into it," said Hiromi. "My friends and I talked about it at school. The ones that get called the wrong name are all the youngest in the family."

"Well, what do you know," Mom said as she attempted to scrub away Kota's paw prints from the tablecloth. "Masahiro's left home, hasn't he? So if I'm going to mistake anyone's name, Hiromi, you're the only one still around."

"What do you mean?" Hiromi shot back with a smile. "You've been doing it since I was a kid. Mistaking me and Kota."

Mom just laughed it off. "I'm going to have to wash this," she said, folding her arms and looking disapprovingly at the tablecloth. "How did Kota learn to do that naughty trick, anyway?" she wondered aloud.

Mom's familiar response, to which Kota wrinkled his nose. *That is no naughty trick. It's a dry run.*

Kota was honing his skills at making paw prints, readying himself for when the time came.

༄

His earliest memory was of being terribly cold. During the rainy season twenty years ago, for whatever reason his mother had left him behind.

His eyes still hadn't fully opened. Crawling out of the space behind a wall where they'd been sleeping, he searched everywhere for the mother cat's warmth. Instead, he was hit by drops of cold, drizzly rain.

In the normal course of things he would have passed away soon after that if he had not been rescued by the father of the Sakuraba family.

The Sakurabas already had a cat: a Persian with an abnormality in its iris that meant the pet shop was about to get rid of it. Mr. Sakuraba had rescued this cat, too. He was the kind of person who, if he crossed paths with a cat in trouble, could not simply walk on by.

So you are one lucky cat, the Persian, named Diana, said, as she let the motherless kitten suck at her teats. Mr. Sakuraba, rather clumsily, often fed him milk, but the need to suck at a warm body with arms and legs like his mother's could not be met by a plastic bottle.

"I want to give him milk, too!" their son, Masahiro, whined.

Diana told the kitten that a human sibling was on its way, and that Masahiro would become an older brother. The pregnant human was in the hospital, she added.

"No. It's too tricky for you to feed him, Masahiro—I'll do it."

This was true, because once when Masahiro tried to feed him a bottle of milk, he stuck the teat so far down the kitten's throat, he coughed for hours afterward.

Apparently while the father was out during the day, he'd

asked Mrs. Sakuraba's friends, women from the neighborhood, to look after him.

He'd been drinking milk every three hours, which became every five hours and then three times a day, by which time the kitten's eyes had fully opened.

It was the day that Mrs. Sakuraba and her new baby, their second son, came home from the hospital.

"Whoa, he looks like a monkey! What a weird face!" Masahiro yelled when he came back from kindergarten, earning a slap from his mother. Diana, though, was inclined to agree with him.

You looked just like a monkey yourself, she thought.

Mrs. Sakuraba had really been looking forward to seeing the kitten her husband had rescued while she was at the hospital. After putting the new baby to sleep, she came over to take a proper look.

"My, what a beautiful silver tabby!"

This was the moment the kitten first learned what his fur color was called.

"Have you decided on a name yet?"

"Not yet," Mr. Sakuraba said a bit evasively.

"But hasn't it been two weeks since you found him?"

"I wasn't sure we were going to keep him, and if we give him a name, then we'll get attached."

Mr. Sakuraba had planned to wait until his wife was back before making a decision about keeping him. But she had no qualms at all.

"Let's adopt him," she said. "The kitten seems to get on well with Diana, too," she added. "You're such a sweet cat now, aren't you, Diana?"

The Persian cat puffed up with pride.

"So, what shall we call him?"

"We need to name the baby first."

A family had to register a baby's name with the city hall within two weeks, and so Mr. and Mrs. Sakuraba had been discussing the matter of the baby's name for quite a while. As the older boy's name was Masahiro, the one thing they'd agreed on was that the new baby's name should contain the same character, *hiro*.

Mr. Sakuraba decided on the name Hiromi, while his wife, after much deliberation, wanted Kota—the *ko* being another reading of the character *hiro*. Neither would back down, and so finally they did rock-paper-scissors to reach a decision. Mr. Sakuraba won.

Mrs. Sakuraba seemed quite disappointed.

"Hiromi . . . isn't a bad choice, but won't people mistake it for a girl's name? I still think Kota might be better."

"No complaints, please. We played for it, fair and square. If you like the name Kota so much, why don't we call the kitten that?"

And that's how he came to be named Kota.

By the time little Kota was scampering around the house, baby Hiromi still had not learned to roll over. All he could do was shuffle his arms and legs around while swaddled in a blanket.

Do you think he's okay? Kota asked worriedly, but Diana reassured him. *Don't worry, he'll be fine.*

Masahiro had been exactly the same, according to her. Humans took longer to grow up than cats.

Even so, it seemed to be taking a very long time. Kota often went to check out little Hiromi as he lay squirming around like a caterpillar.

Wonder if today's the day he'll stand up, thought Kota, fixing him with a good long stare. *Nope, he's still a caterpillar.*

Hurry up and learn to stand. If your mother abandons you, then what? Kota suddenly remembered that his mother had left him behind because he had been such a weak kitten with extremely wobbly hind legs.

One day, as he was nervously scanning Hiromi's sleeping face, the baby's eyes popped wide open.

No one had been able to tell if the baby could actually see anything much, but now those unseeing dark eyes seemed to be focusing at last.

And then he gave a little laugh.

Mrs. Sakuraba came scurrying over.

"I hope you're not trying to bite him," she said.

That's pretty rude, Kota thought, and was about to stalk off, when Hiromi suddenly burst into a loud wailing.

"Hmm . . . Do you want Kota to stay?"

Mrs. Sakuraba patted Kota on the head, and put her hands

together in apology. "I'm sorry. And here you were getting along so nicely."

Ah well, she's the mom, so best to cut her some slack.

Kota nestled down beside the baby's pillow and Hiromi was now all smiles and contented gurgling.

"Isn't that nice, that Kota wants to have a cuddle with you?"

With a heart-melting smile, Mrs. Sakuraba poked at Hiromi's cheeks, and then gave Kota's throat a fond scratch.

Ah, I get it. From the way Mom is smiling, it doesn't look like she's going to get rid of this caterpillar anytime soon. All's well that ends well, Kota thought, giving Hiromi's milky-scented forehead a good lick, thus provoking another happy gurgle of laughter.

Kota began to nestle beside Hiromi every day, until Hiromi learned to roll over and around, then to crawl, then to stand on his own two feet, and finally to walk. Before you knew it, he was racing around the house like a member of some infant biker gang.

He fell down a lot, though, and bumped into things, his motor skills still only half developed. Meanwhile, Kota was fast growing into a full-fledged adult cat.

Humans really do grow up so slowly, he lamented.

You're right, agreed Diana. *By the time the baby reaches Masahiro's age, you could have become an adult five times over.*

When Kota was still a kitten, Masahiro had looked huge to him, but now he seemed like some young kid.

. .

The *fusuma* sliding doors were by this time completely in shreds. They could repaper them all they wanted, but they still ended up in tatters. Mrs. Sakuraba decided to let them stay ripped.

"We have two gangsters in our house," she complained. This was about the time Hiromi was starting kindergarten and Masahiro had gone up to elementary school.

Masahiro was more often now referred to as the *onee*-san—the older brother. Most of the time it was when he was being scolded: "You're the *onee*-san, so you should behave yourself." Masahiro would come back with a sullen, "I hate being the *onee*-san."

"You never tell Hiromi to behave. It's not fair!" he'd protest.

His parents had to admit he had a point.

"Okay, so let's make Hiromi an *onee*-san, too," Mrs. Sakuraba proposed.

"But Hiromi doesn't have a younger brother." Masahiro was pouting again.

"No, but he does have Kota," Mrs. Sakuraba said with a smile.

What? Just a second! Now it was Kota who was getting flustered. *I'm the older brother, actually. I was born first, and besides, I'm already an adult.* But Kota could protest all day—humans couldn't understand cat talk.

"Hiromi, you can be Kota's big brother, can't you?"

"You bet!"

You bet wrong there, little man.

But this cat protest, too, was completely ignored.

You'd best give it up. Humans only understand their own language, Diana said.

"So you'd better set a good example as an older brother for Kota," said Mr. Sakuraba.

Kota dropped his eyes and sat belly down on the floor.

When it comes to walking, running, jumping, even grooming, a kid like Hiromi has absolutely nothing to teach me.

"Before we have dinner, I'd like the two of you to clean up the room, okay? You're both older brothers now, after all."

"Okaay," the two boys answered, a more docile response than usual, and began to gather up the toys and picture books that lay scattered across the floor.

This is how Kota became the third son—*cat*—in the family hierarchy, even though by any measure nothing could have been further from the truth.

ॐ

But now, years later, Hiromi had grown properly big, Kota thought as he gazed up from where he sat at his feet. Hiromi had got up late this morning, but still did not seem to be in a hurry.

Hiromi had grown taller than Mr. Sakuraba, even taller than Masahiro.

"Morning!" Hiromi greeted his mom, who immediately shot back with, "Took your time getting up, that's for sure." Hiromi shrugged. Being a college student seemed a pretty leisurely occupation.

Hiromi gave Kota's head a good pat as he passed by on his way to the fridge. He took out a carton of milk and started to glug it down.

"Don't drink directly from the carton!"

"But I'm going to finish it."

Hiromi drained the milk, rinsed out the carton in the sink and dropped it in the recycling bin.

Aha!

As Hiromi was crouched down arranging items in the recycling bin, Kota, who had been sprawling on the sofa, suddenly saw his chance. He shot over to him and scrambled up Hiromi's back.

"OUCH!!"

By the time Hiromi had let out this overblown yell, Kota was already at his shoulders.

"You scratched my back with your claws, Kota!"

But I have to bare them—how else can I get a grip?

Kota now had a good purchase on Hiromi's shoulders and was gazing down, his face inscrutable. Mrs. Sakuraba, who had been riffling through the morning mail at the dining table, looked over and giggled. "He's never satisfied until he's climbed on top of your shoulders at least once a day."

"Kota has been doing that since he was little. Though it used to be Dad he preferred to climb."

No, you've got that all wrong.

Kota stuck out a paw on the back of Hiromi's neck.

Since he was little. Kota had not been little at all. Only Hiromi and Masahiro had been little at the time. When he'd started to climb up Dad's back, he was already an adult.

"I wonder what it was that made him start that habit."

"Diana never did anything like that, so he's not imitating her."

He did it on purpose, so calling it a habit was a bit annoying. What made him do it? It was Hiromi himself (and Masahiro).

But Hiromi seemed to have forgotten all about it. *He might be big now, but he's still an unreliable little kid, as far as I'm concerned.*

A t the time, the Sakuraba boys were crazy about riding on their dad's shoulders, and whenever their father had a day off, they pestered him.

And as Kota observed the boys in action, he caught on to the rules. The one who got on top of Dad's shoulders was the winner. And it wasn't because he was lifted there.

So a few days later, Kota sat back, quivered his behind as he focused on his target, then took a leap and clambered up Mr. Sakuraba's back. Ignoring Mr. Sakuraba's shouts, Kota kept climbing, grabbing tightly with his claws to the back of his neck, thus winning the cooing admiration of the boys.

Later, Masahiro grew big enough to overtake Mr. Sakuraba, so it was Masahiro he began to climb.

I'm the tallest of all, guys. Cool, right? Who's lowest now, eh?

A few years later Hiromi outpaced Masahiro in height, so Kota switched again. Perceiving how Kota always chose the tallest person to climb, Masahiro wasn't best pleased that the cat was now perching on Hiromi.

"You better get down. You're getting heavy."

As Hiromi tried to pull him off, Kota beat him to the punch and took a deep jump down to the floor, landing in a single beat.

You wish! He had judged the landing perfectly.

"Amazing, amazing," said Mrs. Sakuraba, clapping her hands.

"He's so agile it's hard to believe he'll be twenty this year. And his fur still looks brand-new."

"True. When I took him for shots at the vet's the other day, the people in the waiting room couldn't believe it. A cat with such fluffy fur and he's twenty?"

You're spot-on, Kota thought proudly. *No signs of aging here, thanks very much.*

Pretty soon my tail will show signs of dividing in two.

What about lunch? Will you eat at college?" Mrs. Sakuraba asked her son as he gathered up his books.

"I'll eat before I go."

"Would udon be okay?"

"Sure, anything's fine." Hiromi sat down and began to leaf through the newspaper.

Oh! Kota leaped onto the dining table. Silently stepping across the table, he plunked his behind onto the page that Hiromi was reading.

Hey, how about looking at me instead of that paper? Better on the eyes to gaze at a beautiful gray tabby cat than at all that minuscule writing. And allow yourself to glide your hand down my glossy, fluffy fur.

"*Why* are you squatting right where I'm reading?"

"Diana used to do the same thing." Mrs. Sakuraba smiled nostalgically as she chopped rhythmically with her kitchen knife. From the faint but sharp smell, she was clearly about to top the udon with minced spring onions. Not exactly the kind of thing to tempt a cat.

Diana had taught him that if cats ate spring onions, they'd get sick.

The irresistible smell of dashi stock wafted their way as Mrs. Sakuraba brought in two bowls heaped with udon, a bowl for her and one for Hiromi.

"Here you go."

Kota sauntered off the newspaper and stepped down onto Hiromi's lap. Once Kota had settled down comfortably, Hiromi, as a matter of course, placed his left hand on the cat's spine to hold him.

"That's another strange habit that he's got back into," Mrs. Sakuraba said.

What are you talking about? Kota wasn't sitting on Hiromi's lap because he wanted to. *It was you, Mom, who first told me to sit with Hiromi while he ate.*

This was back when Hiromi was finally old enough to chew his food. He sat in a small chair with a tray attached and often grew bored of sitting and tried to escape, and so Mrs. Sakuraba used to carry Kota over to accompany him at his meal.

"See? Kota's beside you. So be a good boy and eat your food."

She'd picked the right person—scratch that, *cat*—for the job. Since he was a kitten, Kota had slept beside Hiromi every night, and the boy had grown attached to him.

When he got tired of sitting still, Mrs. Sakuraba would pause in feeding him, and let him stroke Kota, and eventually Hiromi no longer tried to wriggle out of the seat.

He can't even eat by himself, Kota thought, a bit stunned, *but if he's this fond of me, I guess I have to pitch in, as part of the family.*

And ever since then, he always sat with Hiromi while he ate.

Around the time Hiromi stopped eating from a tray and began eating at the table, this whole ritual began to fade away, until, in recent years, Kota had felt inclined to revive this duty.

"Doesn't he make it awkward to eat?"

"Not really. Kota's getting old and maybe he's feeling a bit lonely, too."

Okay—go ahead and admit it. It's your habit, not mine—not being able to eat unless I'm with you.

"But eating with one hand doesn't seem polite. You have to figure out another way."

Mrs. Sakuraba said this each time, but had yet to come up with any practical solution. Today, too, Hiromi ate with his right hand, and when he had finished, he tickled Kota's throat.

That's it, right there. A little more to the right.

"Well, I guess I'd better be going." Hiromi stood up and lowered Kota to the floor.

"Just a second—these are yours," Mom said, handing him the letters she'd been sorting through earlier. "You're getting a lot these days."

"It's because I've been applying for seminars and things about job hunting." Hiromi turned over a postcard and frowned. "This one I don't need. An offer from some kind of beauty salon."

"Ah, another person who thinks Hiromi is a girl."

As Mrs. Sakuraba had predicted, people often mistook Hiromi's name for a girl's.

"Around the time of the Adults' Day celebration, you got direct-mail ads for women's kimonos, too."

Hiromi handed the postcard back to his mother. "You can chuck out this one."

"Oh, there's a discount card attached. Can I use it?" she asked.

"Be my guest. Go get all your wrinkles and stuff smoothed out."

"I wonder if it really does help with wrinkles," his mother mused, a serious look on her face as she tugged at her cheeks.

"Hiromi's a nice name and all," Hiromi said, "but I guess there's nothing we can do about other people's mistakes."

His mother stopped tugging at her skin and smiled. "You think it's a nice name?"

"It's okay."

"Tell your dad that next time."

Yeah, Kota agreed. *It would be good to tell him.*

Hiromi gave an awkward smile. "I'll get around to it," he said and gave a little wave as he went out of the door.

∽

I hate the name Hiromi!"

Hiromi had started to whine about his name around the time he started elementary school.

The first time their teacher took the register, he mistook Hiromi for a girl's name.

"Hiromi Sakuraba-chan," he called, adding the *-chan* suffix. But the way he tried to correct his mistake made it even worse.

"Oh, I'm sorry. You're so cute with those long lashes, I mistook you for a girl."

After that, everyone in class would tease him with "Hiromi-*chan*!" His self-respect took a dive.

But the person who was even more upset about it was his dad.

"I just hate the name Hiromi!"

Every time Hiromi threw a tantrum and yelled about his name, Mr. Sakuraba looked about ready to cry, as the choice of name had been his.

"Don't say that," he said. "It's a nice name. One of the characters in Mom's name is in it, too."

Mrs. Sakuraba's name was Akemi, sharing the same character, *mi*, as in Hiromi. For Masahiro they'd taken the *masa* part from Mr. Sakuraba's name, Kazumasa, and he'd decided that for their second son they'd use the same character for *hiro*, and combine it with the *mi* in his wife's name. Mr. Sakuraba had been quite pleased with the choice of name, even before they knew the sex of the baby. "Hiromi will work whether it's a boy or a girl," he said. "We're good either way."

"Maybe Akihiro or Hiroaki would have been good, too." *Aki* being the same character as the *ake* in Akemi. Mrs. Sakuraba chuckled as her husband's face crinkled up tearfully even more.

"At least we should have reversed the characters and named him Yoshihiro," she said. Yoshi being another reading for the character *mi*.

"No way."

She patted her disheartened husband on the head.

"For each of the boys we took one character from your name and one from mine, and both brothers share the character *hiro* in their name, one in the end, one at the beginning. It's clear how we choose names in our family and I think it's a good name."

"NO, IT IS NOT!" Hiromi yelled. "Kota would have been a better name! Let's switch our names!"

Put on the spot, Kota was a bit confused. *Hey, don't involve me in your squabbles, okay?*

"Kota's a boy's name. And Mom wanted to name me Kota when I was born."

His father was so dejected about the whole matter, he finally left the room.

"Oh—*poor Dad*," Masahiro said, exaggeratedly, so they'd take notice. Hiromi felt a little put out, but the next thing his brother said was going too far.

"You're being a bad boy, Hiromi."

"Am not! Let me switch names with Kota!"

"Absolutely not." His mom wouldn't even consider it. "He's been known as Kota for six years, so imagine how much confusion that would cause him to suddenly change names."

"No, it won't. Kota's a cat."

"I don't like it when you say such things—you think because Kota's a cat, you can do whatever you like."

His mother's strict tone got to him, and Hiromi fell silent. When Kota gazed up at them from underneath the chair, Hiromi looked away, teary-eyed.

Thinking maybe she'd gone too far, Mrs. Sakuraba gathered Hiromi up and gave him a cuddle.

"Kota's been called that for six years and taking away a name that has so much love wrapped up in it would be hard for him."

Hiromi still looked unconvinced.

"Your name, too, Hiromi, is filled with six years' worth of love from your family. Do you want to throw away your mother's love for you?"

With her crocodile tears Mom was putting on quite a performance, and Hiromi became suddenly panicked. "No!" he yelled.

Hiromi was yet to be persuaded, but the last thing he wanted was to make his mother cry, so he had to agree.

Humans. I tell you—all this ruckus over a name. Underneath the chair, Kota shrugged. Diana twitched her tail knowingly.

Names, she explained, were very important to humans. Back in the days when they named her, there was quite a commotion between the mother and father.

She herself, she explained, had become the Sakurabas' cat well before Masahiro arrived. His parents had made their decision to name her by rock-paper-scissors back then, too.

Diana was the name of a character in the book *Anne of*

Green Gables that Mrs. Sakuraba favored. But Mr. Sakuraba had suggested something else.

"*Furama?* That's a weird name," was Mrs. Sakuraba's response to her husband's suggestion.

Apparently, it was the name of the hotel they'd stayed at on their honeymoon abroad.

Mr. Sakuraba had rescued Diana just after they'd come home from their honeymoon. He wanted their new cat's name to remind them of their honeymoon, but what his wife most remembered about their hotel was forgetting her keys and locking herself out for hours. Not a pleasant memory, so she had come up with Diana.

Mr. Sakuraba had always been a bit of a romantic.

Just as they had used a character from his name for their eldest son, so he had wanted to include one of the characters from his wife's name for their second—a very sweet and charming gesture.

The evening after Hiromi's crying fit, Mr. Sakuraba went to Hiromi's room, looking as if he'd come to a painful decision. "Here's the thing, Hiromi," he began. "We can't change your name right away, but after you grow up, if you still dislike it, you can apply to the court, and if they give permission, you can change it. So even if you can't do it now, you can consider it when you're older."

Lying curled at the foot of the bed, Kota poked his nose against the soles of Hiromi's feet.

Hey, you're awake, aren't you? Tell him you don't need to change your name. You know it's no big deal—just some friends teasing you.

Hiromi gently pushed Kota's head away with his feet, all the while pretending to be asleep so he wouldn't have to answer his father.

All this commotion over names came to an abrupt halt thanks to their cousin Satsuki-chan, who came to visit during the summer.

Satsuki-chan, who was in the first year of junior high, was a gentle, good-natured girl, and the Sakuraba boys adored her.

Masahiro and Hiromi were continually scrambling around and competing for her attention. As they both vied to show her their good side, they sometimes broke out into a quarrel.

For whatever reason, Masahiro had criticized Hiromi for whining about his name.

"*You're* the one who got upset just because the teacher called you Hiromi-*chan*."

Hiromi turned bright red and started pummeling Masahiro, and soon the boys were rolling around on the floor in a scuffle.

Satsuki-chan intervened and listened to each boy's side of the story in turn. Puzzled, she turned to Hiromi: "Why do you hate your name, Hiromi-kun?"

"Everyone laughs at me because it's a girl's name."

"But I think the name Hiromi is really nice," Satsuki-chan

said, smiling. "When I was in kindergarten, the first boy I liked was called Hiromi. Written with different characters, though."

These words hit Hiromi like a bottom-of-the-ninth, come-from-behind grand-slam home run. Even more so when she told him what a wonderful, handsome boy this first love of hers, Hiromi, had been.

"It's just a coincidence you two have the same first name. Don't think that means she actually likes you, Hiromi!"

Masahiro did his best to dampen Hiromi's good mood, but to no avail.

"Ahh, thank you so much," Mrs. Sakuraba said to her later. "He seemed to really hate it when his friends teased him, and it's still bothering him. And it's made Mr. Sakuraba doubtful as well."

"Well, then, you'd better apologize to your dad," Satsuki said, trying to persuade him.

"Maybe later," Hiromi answered awkwardly.

All this did put an end to Hiromi's crankiness about his name. And to his idea of switching names with Kota.

When the new school term began, his friends seemed to have stopped teasing him. They'd done it because it was fun to get a rise out of him, and now that it didn't seem to bother him anymore, the teasing came to an end.

So Satsuki had helped Hiromi by teaching him how wonderful his name was. And helped his dad, too, after all his brooding over the issue.

It was in the summer of the following year that Satsuki-chan became a helpful influence on the family once again—this time for Kota.

The summer holidays the following year began on a depressing note.

The school's pet rabbit had passed away just before summer break. And it had happened just when Hiromi's class had been looking after it.

Part of their duty involved bringing in vegetables to feed the rabbit, which was one of Hiromi's favorite tasks. The children also vied with each other over who would get to clean out the rabbit hutch. Then, one morning, they discovered their beloved rabbit had given up the ghost, and was now lying stone-cold in the corner of the hutch. The entire school was saddened, but Hiromi's class was especially hard hit.

"Mom, what does *life span* mean?" Hiromi asked when he came back from school that day.

The children were considering holding a class meeting, convinced they'd done something wrong in their rabbit-care duties, but their class teacher had told them that the cause of death was related to *life span*.

"It's no one's fault at all," he'd explained. "The rabbit was old and had reached the end of its life span."

Rather than feeling relieved to hear it wasn't their fault, Hiromi grew concerned about this idea of life span and death.

His mother racked her brain to explain, but Masahiro, entering the rebellious stage, butted in with a mean remark.

"Life span is life span. When you've reached the end of your life span, you die. Didn't you even know that?"

It hadn't been so long ago that Masahiro himself had lost sleep worrying over the same thing.

"Mom, are you and Dad really going to die someday?" he'd asked in the middle of the night, clinging to his mother and crying his little heart out. And now he wanted to act all high and mighty because of all the suffering he'd been through.

"It's not just the rabbit. Kota and Diana, too, will die sooner or later. And also . . ."

"Masahiro!" his mother said angrily and shooed him away. She wanted to get him out of the room before he finished what he was intending to say: *And also Mom and Dad.*

But for Hiromi, the mere thought that Kota and Diana would die like the rabbit was a terrible shock.

"No way!" He burst into tears, for all the world like he had when he was a baby bawling his eyes out. "NO! Kota can't die! Or Diana!"

He yelled Kota's name first, not because he wasn't fond of Diana, but because he and Kota had a special bond. Sure, they were cat and human, but really they were more like brothers. What child, suddenly confronted with the notion that his brother is going to die, wouldn't burst into tears?

Say what you like, Kota thought, *but Masahiro's carried his meanness too far this time*, and he whipped his tail around grumpily and furrowed his brow.

"Don't worry. Kota and Diana are super healthy. They won't die anytime soon."

Mrs. Sakuraba did her best to soothe Hiromi, and after a while he became worn-out from crying and stopped.

But that didn't change the fact that one day Kota and Diana would die. Hiromi was utterly dejected, and that was his emotional state as the summer holidays came around.

There were times when the tears would roll down his cheeks as he slept. And at those times Kota, on his nightly patrols, would press his paws on the boy's cheeks and lick away the tears from either side of his nose.

His heart squeezed, Kota came to Diana. *Tell me*, he asked her as they were sitting under a chair in the living room in the middle of the night. *Is it possible for us to live longer than Hiromi?*

Surely, they just needed to live a single day longer than Hiromi to put an end to his terrible distress.

Unfortunately, I think that may be tricky, said Diana. *If they have a long life, humans can live to nearly a hundred years old. But I've never heard of a cat living that long.*

Can't we do something? I can't stand to see Hiromi feeling so low. It's making me sad.

As the two cats brooded over this, the summer holidays were about to begin and Satsuki-chan would be coming to visit again.

. .

Hiromi liked Satsuki-chan so much, and having her around
did cheer him up, yet still there were times when his face
clouded over and he'd heave a deep sigh.

One day Satsuki-chan was checking the boys' vacation
homework when Hiromi let out a particularly heartfelt sigh.
He didn't seem to be focusing on his homework.

"What's wrong?" That's all Satsuki-chan said, but it was
enough for Hiromi's eyes to fill with tears. They trickled along
those long eyelashes before rolling down his cheeks.

Hiromi explained how the school rabbit had died just before the summer break. He remembered how Masahiro had
said some mean things at the time, but Hiromi was restrained
and didn't say a word about this to Satsuki.

"And Kota and Diana will die someday, too, won't they?"
he asked.

"I suppose so—"

Satsuki-chan tilted her head, baffled as to how best to respond. You couldn't very well expect a second-year junior high
student to give advice on a subject like this.

"But because Kota and Diana are cats . . ."

So what if we're cats? Unconsciously Kota leaned forward at
her words. Diana was doing the same.

"When cats have lived for ten years, they transform completely. Or is it after twenty years?" Satsuki-chan pondered this
question for a time but gave up. "Anyway, they say that if

they're brought up with humans for a long time, they turn into something else."

"*I* know," Masahiro jumped in, having kept quiet all this time. "They change into *nekomata*, like *yokai*, supernatural spirits. And their tails split into two."

"Right, right," Satsuki-chan said, nodding. He'd hit the nail on the head.

Not convinced, Hiromi asked, "So after they become *nekomata*, they can't die?"

"I don't imagine so. Because they're supernatural spirits. I've never heard of spirits dying."

Hiromi's expression brightened, as if discovering light in the midst of unending darkness.

"Diana's already fourteen, isn't she? She's lived a long life, so it might be possible."

"Right?" Satsuki-chan said, seeking Masahiro's agreement. Masahiro, working on his homework, didn't reply.

But at least he didn't deny that spirits actually existed.

"Yay!" Hiromi sprang up, the first genuine smile to break out on his face in weeks.

Now if Kota and Diana could become *nekomata*, then that would solve everything.

But how did you go about becoming a *nekomata*? Did it mean you just had to live a long life and then you could turn into one?

There had to be some procedure, was Diana's opinion.

Whenever there was a change in a human's life, they had to go through procedures at the city hall, she said. Like when someone was born, or they died, or got married. When Masahiro and Hiromi were born, the parents registered their names at the city hall. *You were just a kitten then, Kota, so you might not remember.*

Now that you mention it, Kota said. He was thinking back to when Hiromi was whining about wanting to change his name. His father had told him that to change his name he'd have to apply to the court.

I'm sure that's it, said Diana. When a cat became a *nekomata*, it also had to apply to the city office or court.

But what are they, exactly—these procedures? asked Kota.

There had to be *documents*, Diana said, suddenly brimming with confidence and flicking her ears excitedly. When they sent in Masahiro's and Hiromi's names to the city office, their parents had filled in these documents. Then they had stamped them with their *hanko* seals.

What should we do? We can't write, said Kota.

But even cats can stamp a seal, can't they? Diana replied.

Okay, but where do cats get seals?

This question stumped them for the longest time.

They didn't find a seal in time for Diana.

∽

"I'm back!"

Hiromi had come home from college.

His mother called out from the kitchen, "Good timing. Would you go shopping for me?"

Hiromi put his bag down on the sofa, unable to hide his irritation.

"You should have called or texted me before I got in."

"But I only just remembered I'd forgotten to buy something."

"Okay, okay. So what do you need?"

He might grumble about it, but Hiromi always went along with his mother's requests.

"*Kanikama*—crab sticks."

"Ah—right," Hiromi said, getting it immediately.

"Today's the anniversary of her death."

"So we need to offer some at our altar."

Diana had passed away one winter years earlier, when Hiromi was in elementary school, and *kanikama* had been one of her favorite foods. The day she died, it had been a warm respite from the bitingly cold weather.

"Hard to believe it's been ten years since she passed."

"She lived a long life—sixteen years."

"She could almost have become a *nekomata*."

Hiromi and his mother looked at each other and giggled.

What's this? Kota thought as he sat watching from under the dining table. It had been a long time since they'd mentioned *nekomata*.

Hey, guys, I'm still here, you know.

With that, Kota decided to clamber up Hiromi's back, making him screech in pain and duck his head as Kota dug his front paws into his scalp.

"Not now, Kota. I have to go shopping."

Hiromi lifted his arms to grab him, but Kota slipped from his grasp and lightly, deftly, landed on the floor. He rubbed the top of his head up against Hiromi's knees, and Hiromi, with a resigned smile, scratched him under his chin.

"So you're already twenty-one, aren't you. About time you transformed, I'd say."

Leave it to me. So Diana didn't make it in time, but I've found a hanko *seal.*

Wallet in hand, Hiromi was about to walk out of the living room when he heard his mother's voice. "Oh, one more thing." She had a lot of *one more thing*s when someone was about to leave. "Pick up your suit from the cleaner's. It's ready."

"Oh, you got it cleaned for me? Thanks!"

Hiromi was knee-deep in job searches now and often he'd go out dressed in a suit like his father.

"Hurry now. We'll have dinner as soon as your father gets back."

"Boy, it's one request after another in this place."

Laughing, he headed toward the front door, while Kota trotted at his heels to see him off.

"Don't buy the wrong kind of *kanikama*, now. Diana always liked the low-sodium kind," called his mom.

"Would you like something, too, Kota?" Hiromi patted Kota's head as he headed out, only to return with some of Kota's favorite cod-with-cheese.

ↄ

Diana's congenital eye problem had been getting worse. One eye had become so cloudy she could no longer see out of it. The good eye, too, had got steadily worse and, perhaps afraid of moving around much when her vision was so bad, Diana limited her movements to going to the litter tray or to her food bowl.

That made her appetite drop, and her normally lustrous fur grew matted—she became the very picture of a decrepit cat.

The vet had apparently told them she was reaching the end of her life span.

It's a pity, but it looks like I won't become a nekomata *after all,* Diana murmured as she hobbled around the house. She still hadn't figured out where to get a cat seal. Kota didn't offer any unnecessary words of consolation. Diana's time to live was coming to an end.

Diana could never become a *nekomata.* That was all.

No cat could defy its fate.

Will Hiromi cry his eyes out?

Of course he will. But it's okay—I'll be with him.

I'm counting on you. Diana's voice was low.

.. .

The winter was harsh that year. The moment came when the biting cold was beginning to let up and the sun had begun to shine brightly.

Surrounded by them all as they said their final goodbyes, Diana quietly breathed her last.

I hope you can become a nekomata, *Kota.*

Moments before she died, she uttered these words.

Hiromi cried his eyes out, and did not eat the whole day, but then the next day, as if making up for it, he stuffed himself.

Kota reassured him. *If you eat a lot and sleep well, you'll be fine.*

As he ate a lot and slept well, little by little Hiromi grew bigger, stronger, able to handle more sadness. He no longer teared up at thoughts of missing Diana. Even with her gone, he was able to smile again.

Still, there were nights when he would cry in his sleep.

And Kota would secretly lean his paws on either side of his nose, and lick away those salty tears.

It's okay. I'm here with you. I'll become a nekomata *and watch over you, Hiromi.*

This was what Diana had wanted.

A *hanko* seal, a seal, a cat seal. So where did you get hold of this cat seal, the kind you needed to carry out the procedure of becoming a *nekomata*?

All of a sudden, he found it.

.. .

I f you could stamp your seal here, please."

It's what the package delivery boys always said.

Mrs. Sakuraba kept the seal for deliveries near the front door, stamping it onto a receipt before taking in the package.

On that particular day, the seal was missing and she couldn't find it anywhere.

"Can I just do a fingerprint?" Mrs. Sakuraba asked the delivery boy.

"Sure."

She touched her index finger to the red ink pad and pressed it against the receipt.

From below, Kota watched the whole process with great interest.

How to put it? He'd found the bluebird of happiness, right here, in his own house.

A cat's seal was right here, in the paw he'd been born with.

Now that he knew, all that remained was to practice. Sometimes he saw Mrs. Sakuraba mess up stamping a seal and being forced to redo it.

To avoid this, he'd have to master the art of stamping his print. And so Kota diligently went about practicing paw prints.

Whenever Mrs. Sakuraba left the red ink pad out, Kota jumped at it, and whenever Mr. Sakuraba was stamping a template greeting onto his New Year cards, Kota stretched out his paw into the red ink and stamped his print onto the pristine white cards.

"KOTA!" Mr. Sakuraba roared.

"It's okay," his wife said. "You can pretend they're plum blossoms." She took out a calligraphy pen and added some branches.

Kota found lots of things worked for practicing paw prints: the paints Hiromi used for art, spilled ketchup, and, yes, soy sauce, even though it wasn't red.

The only thing he needed now was the document.

One day soon, while sorting through the mail, Mrs. Sakuraba would surely say, "Kota, this one's yours," and pass him a document.

∽

After a long job search, Hiromi finally decided to take a job at a travel agency. Whenever he helped organize trips for his club at college, he found he enjoyed it more than he'd expected.

On the day he received the still-unofficial job offer, the family celebrated, and even though it wasn't exactly the anniversary of Diana's passing, they placed some of her favorite *kanikama* in front of her photo. Kota got some delicious chicken jerky to eat.

Masahiro wasn't there that day, but when he and his wife next came to visit, he brought a necktie as a present for his brother, to celebrate his new job.

His parents, naturally, also gave Hiromi a present. Mr.

Sakuraba gave him a wristwatch, while Mrs. Sakuraba gave him a baby-carrier sling.

Hiromi eyed it dubiously.

"What's this?"

"A sling. You use it like this." She slung it diagonally across her body and placed Kota inside it. "It's really to carry a baby with, but a cat fits, too. Use this and you'll have both hands free, especially at mealtimes."

"Makes sense. It's useful for sure. But is this really a present for me? Not for Kota?"

"I've been thinking about a solution for ages. And I happened to find this."

"Well, I guess it's okay."

During meals, Hiromi now placed Kota in the sling, keeping him close to his chest and freeing up his hands.

"But what a strange cat he is," his dad said. "A climbing cat, who also paints, and now that he's old, a cat you carry around."

"He might soon start walking around on two legs," added his mom.

"And finally turn into one of those magical cats."

Hiromi smiled and patted Kota's forehead, which was poking out of the sling.

"Do your best to be a *nekomata*."

Satsuki-chan, who'd first told him about *nekomata*, still phoned regularly. She'd taken a job at a company in her hometown and was even training the new employees.

Winter arrived, and so, too, the anniversary of Diana's passing, and then spring.

Hiromi began commuting to work wearing a suit.

"See you later!" he called, but his mom stopped him.

"You missed a spot shaving," she said, tapping her own chin. Hiromi ran back to the bathroom and picked up his electric shaver.

Oh, his back is wide open!

Kota quivered his tail in preparation to climb, but Hiromi, noticing at the last minute, dodged aside. The jump failed to launch.

"Don't do that. I'm wearing a suit. It'd be awful if you rip it."

This newly ordered suit wasn't like the shirts and sweatshirts he was used to wearing.

Okay, I'll let it slide this time. But two times out of three, I'll look for my chance.

Hiromi began to get used to Kota climbing up him even when he had a suit on, and had started to shave with Kota squatting on his shoulder.

Mom—could you make *tonkatsu* for dinner tonight?" Hiromi asked one day as he was coming in from work. This was in the autumn, and he'd been at the travel agency for six months.

"How come? Do you have a test coming up?"

Hiromi had never been picky about his food, so he didn't

usually make requests like this—the only time being when he had an important exam, and then he'd ask for *tonkatsu*, or deep-fried breaded pork cutlets, considered lucky since the word *katsu* was a homonym for "win."

But he'd already graduated from college.

Looking up from below, Kota tilted his head, puzzled, until Hiromi revealed what was up.

"Yeah, I have a qualifying exam at work."

Come to think of it, he had been staying up late these days, studying, thought Kota.

His mother did her very best to make a nice meal of *tonkatsu*. When Kota was about to use the leftover sauce in a dish for his seal-stamping practice, Mrs. Sakuraba screeched, *"Stop that!"* and Hiromi and his dad managed to block him.

The next morning, Hiromi set off for his exam in high spirits.

About a month later, Mrs. Sakuraba was sorting through the mail. "Oh!" she called out. "Is this a notification about the exam?"

She waited nervously until Hiromi got home, then did her best to hand him the notification calmly.

Looking tense, Hiromi opened the envelope.

Either because of his mother's *tonkatsu* or perhaps because of Hiromi's own efforts, he'd passed with flying colors.

Kota looked askance as the parents whooped it up in celebration and instead placed his nose on the document to give it a sniff. *Don't you stamp a seal on this document?*

"What's the matter, Kota? You going to read it?"

No, I was just wondering why it's taking so long for my document to come.

Thinking, mistakenly, that Kota was interested in his notification, Hiromi explained its contents to him.

"This means I'm qualified to escort tours abroad."

"When will your first escort job be?" his mother asked, to which Hiromi shook his head.

"Who knows," he said. "The soonest people can escort a tour seems to be after their first year with the company."

He seemed excited, wondering when the first assignment would come, and what country it would take him to.

Winter arrived, and so, too, the anniversary of Diana's passing, and spring was now on its way.

The following took place on one of those days before spring.

Hiromi was at the sink, shaving.

His back is wide open!

Kota jumped, trying to scramble up, but then—

Oh gosh, what's wrong?

He suddenly found himself falling off. Hiromi turned around, gazing down at him in shock.

Couldn't do it—must be an off day for me. Feeling awkward, Kota scuttled away.

From that day Kota could no longer climb up Hiromi's back. He tried over and over, but could never manage it. Not only that, but he could no longer leap up onto the dining table. He had to jump onto the chair first.

The condition of old age that had caught up with Diana seemed to be grabbing hold of Kota as well.

I guess I was a bit too complacent, since Satsuki-chan had said that if I ever reached twenty, I'd become transformed.

And here was Kota, aged twenty-three. The next rainy season, he'd turn twenty-four.

He'd been so positive that once he got to this age, he'd become a *nekomata*.

But Kota's document never arrived.

After all that practice stamping my print.

Spring was around the corner. The cold snaps and warmer breezes contended with each other, the temperature fluctuating day by day. There would be three cold days, followed by four warm ones, and in the midst of this, Kota carelessly caught a cold. His eyes became coated with an unusual film and Mrs. Sakuraba took him hurriedly to the vet's.

The vet put eyedrops in, but the cold lingered and Kota's strength began to fade.

I get it. I don't have long to go.

Just then, Hiromi's first foreign tour came through.

"Where is it?"

"France. A tour around Mont-Saint-Michel."

"That's wonderful! You wanted to go there, didn't you," his mom said, but it was clear she was forcing herself to sound cheerful.

"Yes, I really did. But why *now*?"

"It can't be helped. If you tell them you can't go because you're worried about your cat, they'll fire you."

Mrs. Sakuraba used a pipette in the corner of his mouth to feed Kota his medicine. At first he struggled mightily, but then he gave in and let her have her way.

If I waste time struggling, the little time I have left will slip away.

"It'll be okay. It's only one week, isn't it? I'm sure he'll wait for you."

His mom might have said this, but her heart told her otherwise.

No one believes it, but I believe in myself. I can hold out until Hiromi comes home.

"So go and enjoy your trip. How can a cat who's lived twenty-three years not hold out one more week?"

Hiromi caressed Kota's fluffy fur, as if this was their final farewell, then he set out on his tour.

He called home every day. Morning and night.

Sometimes the phone would ring just before dawn, and his mother would answer, never sounding annoyed.

"Don't worry. He's taking his medicine the way he should."

Masahiro, who lived far away, came one time to see how Kota was doing.

"I think this is the end," he said before getting back in his car regretfully and driving home in the middle of the night.

One night. Two nights. How many days has it been?

Waves of gentle drowsiness kept washing over Kota, over and over.

If I were engulfed by these waves, I would probably never wake up again.

But I'm not afraid. Because it's the place where Diana went.

Everyone goes there eventually. Father will, and Mother, and Masahiro . . . and Hiromi, too.

It's a shame I can't be here to see Hiromi on his way. After how Satsuki-chan told me about becoming a nekomata *and all.*

And here I am, so expert at making a paw-print seal.

I only wish I could have outlived Hiromi—even by a single day.

But Hiromi's all grown up now. Big and strong, the tallest one in the family. So tall, I can't climb up him anymore.

So he'll be fine.

With that healthy body, he can surely handle any amount of sorrow.

Another wave of drowsiness swept over him.

Suddenly a large hand stroked his head. Fingers tickled at his throat and slipped behind his ears to scratch.

A purr came out on its own.

Stop it, I'll feel so good it'll make me sleep. And I won't be able to wake up.

Kota.

He felt like Hiromi was calling him.

Hiromi.

Hiromi, Hiromi. Hi-ro-mi.

It's a nice name. So what if your friends teased you. No big deal.

The masa *in Masahiro comes from your father's name, the* mi *in Hiromi from your mother's. And you and Masahiro both share the* hiro *part. It's like that game where you make a new word from the last syllable of the previous one.*

And my name, too, has the same character for hiro *in it. We're a matching set.*

There is no other name that could connect you so completely to your family.

So, come on, go and tell your dad what a great name it is.

⌒

H is father went to the airport to fetch him.

They took the highway and were home within the hour.

"Go now," his father said, and Hiromi opened the door and rushed into the house before his father parked the car in the garage.

The front door was unlocked; he kicked off his shoes and ran in.

They'd made Kota's bed in the living room, in the warmest spot.

Mrs. Sakuraba was tending him, her eyes swollen from crying.

"Is he still . . . ?"

She nodded. Still alive.

Hiromi came closer. Trembling, he knelt down and, with the tips of his four fingers, started to stroke the little silver tabby head.

He tickled his throat and scratched behind his ear.

And Kota purred.

"Kota."

The voice croaked. Kota, too, gave a feeble, hoarse meow.

The family had all taken turns stroking him, over and over, coaxing an occasional brief purr.

Near dawn the purrs suddenly stopped.

"Oh. I thought he was asleep—"

But he'd passed, and never purred again.

Hiromi was not sure why, but he didn't feel sad.

Just grateful.

"He waited for you, Hiromi."

His mother's voice was gentle.

"So your first big job wouldn't be a sad memory."

His father laughed.

"A climbing cat, a drawing cat, a carried cat and, to the very end, a considerate cat. A cat of many talents, for sure."

"*Dad.*"

He didn't know why it happened then, at that moment. But the words spilled out, as if he had to get them out.

"My name is really nice."

"What's this all about?"

"I really do think it's nice."

He gently stroked Kota's still-warm body.

"Even if I were reborn, I'd want to be your child. And be named Hiromi and bring Kota up all over again."

"You're leaving out Masahiro," his mom teased.

"If he asks me, I'll let him be my older brother."

And if Hiromi asked his older brother, he would surely let him be his younger brother.

"So name him Masahiro again, and name me Hiromi."

"Sure. That sounds good, I guess . . ."

Bringing Up Baby

When Kaori Tsukuda came home from her parents' house, where she'd gone to stay when she was about to give birth, she found something major had happened in her absence.

Her husband, Keisuke, had stayed behind to take care of their home while she was gone. Keisuke, under the name *Keisuke Tsukuda*, written in katakana, was a midlevel manga artist who contributed to a monthly boys' magazine. A few years before, he'd had a hit series, but ever since then he had been confined to one-shot manga or short-term series, toiling away as the epitome of a steady cartoonist.

He was, from the outset, the type of person who put his heart and soul into manga. The manga world was a harsh one, though, and you could give it everything you had and still never have any success. Kaori had laid down the law before she went to her parents' place: use the opportunity to sharpen his domestic side, she told her husband, though she didn't really expect the house to be shipshape when she got back.

Keisuke was supposed to collect her today at the Ueno station, but just before she got off the Shinkansen train, he had called, apologizing profusely for not being able to make it. He didn't have any looming deadlines, as far as she recalled, but with someone so completely dedicated to manga, this was nothing new. With his wife away for a month, it was probably beyond him to straighten up the now messy, cluttered house in a single day. This was a man who kept putting off his manga assignments, so expecting him to handle a household on his own was a total pipe dream.

With the baby to carry and still not feeling a hundred percent, she decided to grab a taxi from the station.

Before she'd left home, she'd arranged for all the baby-related items she'd need. The only thing Keisuke had to do was assemble the crib before they returned, and she'd made it emphatically clear that if he didn't, he was a dead man. As long as he took care of this single task, she figured his life would be mercifully spared.

They lived in an odd house that they'd managed to acquire when Keisuke had his hit series. They knew they couldn't let the chance slip by and scraped together as big a deposit as they could.

When Kaori got home and rang the front bell, her husband wasn't in. Maybe he'd stepped out to the local convenience store? She opened the front door with her own key.

She steeled herself for an appalling sight, but when she actually stepped inside, the house was a bit dusty, for sure, and there were opened cardboard boxes randomly piled up in the hallway, but overall the place was in decent order.

The cardboard boxes were mainly baby goods Kaori had ordered. Milk, diapers, baby wipes, a litter tray for a cat . . .

Wait, what?

She did a double take, but nothing had changed. A cardboard box that had held a cat-litter tray was right there, as clear as day.

Just then, the front door clicked open behind her.

"Oh . . ."

She turned, and when their eyes met, her husband let out a guilty little yelp.

In one hand, he held a bag. No, not a bag, exactly, but a carrier for an animal. Out of which issued a siren-like wail.

"What on earth is—*that*?!" Kaori squealed, and the baby in her arms joined in the wailing.

∽

Their baby's name was Shiori.

Keisuke had named her.

They'd agreed from the beginning that Keisuke would choose the baby's name. Otherwise, Kaori felt he'd remain forever an unreliable cartoonist focused solely on his work. When she first told him she was pregnant, he just looked vacant, and it was impossible for her to tell if he was happy or not.

On top of that he'd asked, "Is it mine?" and war broke out between them. She'd fired off an instant "I want a divorce!" machine-gun burst; Keisuke had yelled out, "Mayday! Mayday!" and that was the extent of their *hostilities*.

"No—*no*, that's not what I meant," Keisuke kept on saying, repeating himself like a broken record.

Kaori, exhausted by her anger, asked, "If that's not it, then *what*?"

To which he snapped, "I just can't believe it."

"Okay, then we'll get divorced," she replied, and laughed almost sneeringly at him.

He waved his hand. "No, you don't understand."

"Don't understand *what*?"

Keisuke said something along the lines of not being able to believe that he was going to be a parent. Or at least she thought so. She'd been so upset that now she couldn't really recall his exact words.

"I couldn't believe someone as hopeless as me was going to be a parent," he explained over and over through his tears. A complaint you might very well expect from Keisuke, whose whole life was manga and who tended to be a bull in a china shop in any social situation.

∿

All I do is draw manga, but I'm involved in tax evasion? Me?"

When his big hit series came out and his income skyrocketed, Keisuke was so pressed by work that he forgot to submit his latest income tax return. But the fact remained that he'd let it slip and had therefore defaulted on paying a hefty amount of tax.

At the time, Kaori, who worked as an editor at the same publishing company, had been selected as the personal assistant to Keisuke, in charge of managing his affairs, and her very first task was to find an accountant to resolve this nonpayment problem.

"Paying taxes is the duty of every citizen. *Comprenez-vous?*" said Kaori.

Having the writer of their signature series involved in tax evasion was a blow to the publishing company's reputation. They could replace his series with another, but there was no stand-in for a scandal. *Whatever you do, get him to pay his back taxes* was the eyes-only order that came down from the company president.

After that, she didn't receive a single manga manuscript from him. Kaori's job now as personal assistant in charge of him meant dealing with the accountant, her tasks entailing such things as unearthing utility bills and receipts for necessary expenses from his workplace and getting them in some kind of order, as well as the extra task of keeping an account book of his expenses.

Around this time the accountant urged them to file an income tax return, and when she reported this to Keisuke, he said, "For goodness' sake," and left it all up to her. Kaori had to devise a company name for him and submit a notification of his business opening. Around the time the manga series was reaching its grand finale, Kaori was transferred to a different section within the publishing company. The accounting department. Considering what she'd achieved as personal assistant for *Keisuke Tsukuda*, it made sense.

When he heard she was going to continue to be in charge of his accounts, Keisuke grew pale and apologized to her in tears. Turning on the tears was SOP for him, in all kinds of situations.

"I don't get why you're making me in charge of a company all of a sudden," he said.

"How dare you say that! You're the one who created this mess, and I was the one who had to clean it all up."

She didn't owe him anything, she thought, so she could have just slugged him and left. But just as these feelings welled up, Keisuke told her, *I don't know what I'd do without you.* And this led to a proposal to *Marry me*, which only reinforced what an idiot he was when it came to social interactions.

Even so, for her there was none of that starry-eyed *I love you more than ever* type of development.

Except—

Kaori had really liked the *Keisuke Tsukuda* manga and had read them even before his big hit series.

Throughout the years she'd been working as his personal assistant, she'd seen how socially inept he was, and was sure that if she stepped aside, the time would come when he would be ruined financially. For one reason or another—nonpayment of taxes or tax evasion, or perhaps because a friend or some woman had tricked him out of his savings. Whatever the reason, it was inevitable.

If that happened, she wouldn't be able to read his manga anymore, she thought, which would be a great shame.

And that thought made her blurt out, to his sudden marriage proposal, "Sure, if you like me . . ." And the deed was done.

Someone like me can be a dad?" he'd asked.

Keisuke's tears continued to flow. *It isn't a question of* can you, *pal*, she thought. *You're* going *to be one and that's that.*

In the end, her response boiled down to just two words: *Be one.*

Keisuke may have noticed how worked up she was—that she would only accept *Yes!* as an answer—and so he nodded his assent.

But her pregnancy went by with no visible change in him, Keisuke still his usual undependable self. His seed had been sown and taken root, but that wasn't enough to him, she concluded.

When their daughter was born and Kaori was in the maternity hospital, Keisuke seemed less moved by the experience than a little afraid. Out of a sense of awe for a new life? Maybe that would explain his reaction to becoming a father.

At least he could be given the task of naming the baby, she decided. The way he'd incorporated the character *ri* from her name, Kaori, into the baby's, Shiori, was something a father might come up with, and she was impressed. Kaori's parents, and Keisuke's, too, praised him to the moon for coming up with it. The unspoken understanding being that praising him might finally help him grow up.

Please be patient with him, her parents-in-law had said, asking her to take good care of him. And she planned to—but still she thought, *Shiori, your papa is a harder nut to crack than I reckoned.*

∽

"What's going on here?"

Kaori had given milk to the crying Shiori and put her to sleep in the bouncer in the living room, and now was the time to face each other.

"Right . . . so, can I let it out?"

The kitten inside the carrier, is what he meant. It was an orange tabby cat. Its nose was pink, so the pads of its feet were probably pink, too. Kaori was familiar enough with cats to deduce this much from a quick glance. They'd always had cats when she was growing up, and even now her parents had one.

"Keep it shut."

Now that they were in the same room, she knew she'd lose her resolve if the cat started wandering around.

"Until when?"

When, where, who, what, why, how? At this point the only answered questions were *who* and *what*. *When, where, why* and *how* had Keisuke picked up a stray cat?

"Well . . . it was about three weeks ago, maybe?"

Hey—you've been keeping it that long! she was about to yell, but stopped at *Hey*, seeing how it made Keisuke flinch and, her common sense working, realizing she might wake Shiori.

"Where?"

"The rubbish recycling point."

The local recycling center was diagonally opposite their house. What trap lay in wait in the space of just a few dozen meters?

"Because you told me never to let the kitchen waste pile up."

Three weeks ago, Keisuke had, at Kaori's insistence that the rubbish not pile up, picked up a cat.

Wait a second—that doesn't make sense.

"I went to dispose of the rubbish and I spotted a cat that'd been thrown away."

"You don't have to use that *Never let the kitchen waste pile up* line anymore. It has nothing to do with it."

"It was in a Mikkabi brand tangerine box."

An amazing memory for detail.

"I was the very first one to take out the rubbish."

Keisuke tended to be a night person, so it was easiest for him to take the rubbish out early in the morning after he'd stayed up all night. That way he wouldn't forget.

"As I was the first to arrive, the Mikkabi tangerine label kind of leaped out at me. I thought, *Hey, today's not the day for recyclable waste.* I wondered if it was okay to leave it out like that."

Amazing that he'd remembered the waste collection schedule, and she couldn't help but feel a few tears well up at how he was awakening—at long last—to what society expected of him.

"I thought, *Hmm, maybe I should flatten the box*."

The kind of consideration an adult would show, but hard to say if that was good or bad. It wouldn't do to have others think he'd been the one to violate the rules about what kind of rubbish went out on which day, but adult wisdom dictated that he cluck his tongue, make a face and let it pass. How things worked normally in their neighborhood was that, in a case like this, if someone else showed up, you should say something like, "Isn't it nonrecyclable waste today?" and just ignore the tangerine box so that when the rubbish truck arrived and slapped a *Cannot Be Picked Up* label on the box, leaving it behind, the person who'd left it would realize his mistake and take it back.

In any event, Keisuke, wanting to display a Good Samaritan spirit, was about to crush the tangerine box.

"I thought, *Hey, there's still a couple of tangerines inside*, but when I looked, it turned out that one was a marmalade kitten, and the other was a tiny black one that looked a bit like a moldy tangerine . . ."

"They call that a rust pattern."

"The kittens' eyes weren't open yet, and the rust-patterned one was already cold. It was probably too small to have been able to survive. So I brought the other one back home for the time being and thought I'd take it to a vet."

The vet took care of the dead kitten. He instructed Keisuke on how to feed the other one with milk and how to deal with its waste. Its fur was clean, with no fleas or ticks, so it seemed like it'd been a house pet and then discarded. Maybe the kittens had been too much for the mother cat to cope with.

"The vet said that if it were a stray, it'd be full of fleas and ticks by now, since its sibling had died before it."

When a host dies, fleas and ticks immediately move to another host. And here the destination might have been the warm little orange tabby in the same box.

"The vet said to bring it in when it's weaned, for a blood and stool test."

Weaned? What are *you talking about?*

"When your own daughter is still an infant?" Kaori asked incredulously.

Back at her parents' home, they'd waited on her hand and foot, but now it was all up to her and she wasn't sure what to do. Add to that managing their home every day, a husband with few social skills—and now an unweaned kitten? It was all too much.

Inside the carrier, the kitten meowed and started to scrape at the lid. *Let me out, let me out.*

For goodness' sake, I can't think straight.

"Two unweaned infants—it's like some impossible game . . ."

"It's not two. Spin's already eating solid food . . ."

"What the—you've already *named* it? Give it a name and you'll grow attached to it. That's a problem. So why do you think I put you in charge of naming Shiori? Anyway, we need to find someone to take it."

Taking the kitten to her parents' was a last resort. They

used to have two cats, and now only had one, so there was an opening. It'd be a problem if the cats didn't get along, but they could always keep them in separate rooms if they had to.

Mention of someone else taking Spin had Keisuke protectively shifting the carrier behind him. The hands can be as eloquent as the mouth.

"I . . . I thought if I abandoned it, I wouldn't be qualified anymore."

"What do you mean, *qualified*?"

"I mean, Shiori's been born and all . . ." He looked at her pleadingly. "I thought, *Shiori's been born now, but if I abandon this little kitten, I couldn't be a parent.*"

You didn't have to take it in—it wasn't necessarily going to die. But that was too much sophistry and she couldn't voice it. The sibling kitten in the Mikkabi tangerine box, the rust-colored one, had indeed died.

If he'd abandoned this orange tabby, it would have died and he'd be the one who'd left it to its fate. Having the mindset to come up with such a compelling story with such speed was what made Keisuke Tsukuda *Keisuke Tsukuda*. The kind of story where you relied on others—where someone else was sure to rescue the kitten if you didn't—that would never make a convincing manga. It was the mindset of a person who'd take the initiative and crush the box. A person who wasn't a hero would have nothing to do with the tangerine box and would therefore not discover the kittens inside.

"It's a Schrödinger's Kitten, isn't it," said Keisuke.

Until the kittens were actually observed, it was unclear if they were dead or alive. If Kaori had been the one taking out the rubbish that day, she would have followed the waste collection rules and never noticed them, and the cat would never have existed as part of the Tsukuda household's *universe*.

Keisuke Tsukuda, though, did observe the kitten and even gave it a name, so the kitten in the Mikkabi tangerine box became a fixed part of the Tsukuda family.

Show the same mindset when it comes to Shiori, okay? Otherwise you're dead.

"Why weren't you here when we arrived?"

"I had to pick it up at the vet . . . they called me."

It goes without saying that Keisuke at this point was blubbering. His emotions fluctuated so wildly that what he said had to be true.

"Yesterday morning, Spin started vomiting."

Cats were creatures who did a lot of vomiting—vomiting after eating, after drinking, vomiting up hairballs—but when a little kitten vomited, it was scary.

"I checked and it had chewed an eraser, and there was part of an eraser mixed in with the vomit."

That required going to the vet.

"They did an X-ray and an ultrasound but didn't find any foreign object inside. I checked the piece of eraser the cat had vomited with the original eraser and I think it had vomited up everything. The vet told me that if there's any left, it'll come out in the cat's stool, but advised me to keep it there overnight for observation. And I just got the call a while ago saying that it was fine and to come pick the cat up."

Keisuke's shoulders shook with a sob.

"I . . . if it had died, I don't know what I'd . . ."

He broke down, crying, and didn't finish the thought.

Piecing together his broken words between the sobs, Kaori realized he was saying that it had been his fault for leaving the eraser out.

It was true that he'd never taken care of a pet before. If the kitten happened to die on him, it would be like a giant hatchet had split apart his hero's sensibility.

The orange tabby kitten was scratching at the gaps in the carrier.

Good thing you're a strong cat, you.

"I'm sorry I couldn't pick you guys up at the station."

"Well . . . I guess it couldn't be helped. Its name is *Spi*—?"

"Spin."

"Spin? Like turning, rotating?" She rotated a finger, asking him how he'd come up with the name. Was it connected to the way a cat would spin round and round chasing a toy?

"Exactly."

Keisuke pointed at a book on the low table. One of Kaori's books.

I remember—I was reading it just before I left the house, she thought. It'd been lying there a whole month and he hadn't put it away?

"When the kitten first opened its eyes, the first thing it

played with was the ribbon *shiori*—the bookmark—in that book."

There was a blue ribbon bookmark peeping an inch or two out of the bottom of the book.

"It kept on batting at it. It was so cute."

"Then let that cute thing out."

As Keisuke opened the carrier, the orange tabby batted at Keisuke's hand. Keisuke seemed used to this.

As Kaori picked up the kitten, she realized it had been decades since she'd felt this kind of soft, downy fur. Below the forlorn little butthole, which looked like a small line made on clay with a tiny spatula, there were no fluffy little cat balls.

"So it's . . . female?"

"Good catch."

"But doesn't Spin sound more like a boy's name?"

"But she's Shiori's little sister." She was playing with the *shiori* bookmark.

So when he'd named the cat, thoughts of Shiori had indeed crossed his mind. For Keisuke this was quite an achievement.

"Shiori, look. It's your little sister!"

He held up the kitten and swung her toward Shiori's pillow. Spin gave the baby's head a gentle sniff. Spin had soft downy hair, and so did Shiori.

Perhaps because Shiori had a milky odor, Spin began to purr and groom Shiori's soft hair.

Shiori woke up, her eyes swiveling toward the kitten. She shouldn't be able to see properly yet, but she did seem to be staring at Spin. She shouldn't be able to smile yet, either, but she seemed somehow to be smiling.

The two of them seemed to hit it off well.

One reason the house had been cleaned up more efficiently than Kaori had anticipated was so that Spin wouldn't mistakenly swallow something she shouldn't. The vet had drilled into Keisuke's head how dangerous it was for cats to eat something they shouldn't, and Keisuke told her how while Spin was at the vet's he'd stayed up all night tidying up the house to avoid history repeating itself.

"When I was cleaning up, I came across all kinds of things on the floor that Spin might accidentally swallow. If she swallowed, say, a piece of string, the vet told me they'd have to operate and cut open her stomach."

Kaori suddenly noticed that the Lego and plastic models that had been piled up on the sideboard in the living room were now stored away in a clear plastic case. Many were the times she'd cut her foot when she stepped on a fallen piece, and she'd told him to either put them away or get rid of them, and had bought him the plastic case. But for years the case had just sat there, gathering dust.

One little cat could convince him when a million rants from his wife could not. *Well*, she thought, *I can live with that.* Was there a woman, or a man, in this world who could beat a cat?

"And the things that Spin might swallow, Shiori might as

well. So I thought I'd better straighten up the house before Spin and Shiori came home."

Goodness. What had happened to the Keisuke she knew? When it came to the cat, he'd got the master–servant relationship backward but had worked out, nonetheless, that what was dangerous for Spin would be equally dangerous for Shiori.

"All that's left is to vacuum," Keisuke said, getting to his feet. He was even taking the initiative when it came to housework.

"The floor wiper should be enough. You'll wake Shiori."

After Spin had raked her claws softly a few times through Shiori's downy hair, the baby had fallen asleep again in the baby bouncer.

"Good point. Spin would be frightened, too."

Kaori suddenly thought of something.

"Now, did *I* buy that bouncer?"

She recalled that when she'd been checking out all the baby-related goods she'd need, she'd put it lower on the list since it might not be used all that long.

"Oh, I bought that. I figured if Spin's running around, she might step on Shiori."

After Spin's eyes had opened, she'd become more active and mischievous, Keisuke explained. "It came a couple of days ago and I assembled it. I'm glad it arrived in time."

"Now you're acting like a proper human being!" The words just slipped out.

Keisuke smiled in embarrassment.

Should he feel embarrassment at this moment? Kaori wondered. Wouldn't most people feel offended?

"I don't want Spin or Shiori dying or getting injured."

Again the master–servant relationship had the cat on top. But that was okay. Nothing to worry about. What keeps the cat safe keeps the baby safe. And what keeps the baby safe keeps the cat safe. Two sides of the same coin. Yin and yang. A safe, happy family.

As Keisuke started to wipe the floor, Spin began to meow. *Right*—this *cry I recognize*, Kaori thought, wondering if the kitten had been fed.

"What about Spin's food?" she asked.

"It's in a drawer underneath the oven. It's in pouches, and I take out half a pouch and warm it up a bit. You're smart to know she's hungry!" Keisuke added, eyes wide.

"She sounds just like Shiori when she's hungry. The same sort of crying."

Maybe because they couldn't speak, the urgent need in their tone struck you all the more.

Kaori went out to the kitchen and Spin skipped through after her. She didn't seem in the least bit shy. Maybe because she knew she was a member of the family? Animals and babies are said to pick up on the relationship with new people from the vibe they get from other family members.

Spin's matching food and water bowls and her litter tray were lined up neatly along the floor in the kitchen, proof of how determined Keisuke had been to keep the kitten.

Spin's little tail described a figure eight as it brushed against Kaori's feet, then stuck straight up, the tip quivering. A happy tail. There were all kinds of tails on cats—long ones, short ones, hooked ones. All good, but longer tails were more expressive.

When Spin smelled the warmed-up food in her bowl, her purring moved up a gear and she was all over it. Maybe she'd been too tense at the vet's to eat anything.

Seen from above, the head and body were like two downy balls, with two triangles for the ears attached to the smaller ball. Any way you looked at it, this was a miraculous creature—a winner of a Good Design award. She wouldn't be a kitten much longer; crouching over the little cat, Kaori found she could study her forever.

"This won't do—I'm wasting time."

She shook off the spell and stood up.

"I'm going to go crush those cardboard boxes in the entrance," she announced, and was heading in that direction when Keisuke stopped her.

"No, I'll do it," he said. "The Shinkansen train must have been tiring. You go and lie down, and I'll let you know if Shiori starts crying."

He really had become more human, she mused, even shivering a little at the thought.

Taking him at his word, she headed to the bedroom. The setup there had changed in her absence. Immediately inside, along the wall, was the crib, and in order to accommodate it, their own two beds had been shifted to face in a different direction from before. An adjustment of the layout done with the logistics of baby care in mind.

Assemble the baby's crib. Otherwise, you're a dead man! He'd not only passed the test, but had done so in medal-worthy fashion.

The bedclothes seemed untouched since Kaori had left, the pillowcase retaining her scent, but that was trivial. She'd got the bed because taking out futons and then storing them away every day was a pain, and she wasn't proud of how seldom even she changed the sheets. Once while she was chatting with people at work, the topic of how often they changed the futon covers had come up, and she was in the corner that hemmed and hawed about it, before beating a hasty retreat.

Not long after she had got into bed, she heard the soft padding of feet approaching. She'd been wondering when the kitten would come. Sensing a presence near her bed, she lifted her head before the feet pattered away again.

The feeling of having a tiny living creature moving about the house as it pleased filled her with a surprising warmth. Perhaps because it had been so many years since she'd had a cat in her life.

And, she thought, being brought up with that warm little creature maybe wouldn't be such a bad thing for a baby.

She trimmed Shiori's fingernails every day. A baby's nails were like thin razor blades, and if you let them grow out even a little, they'd tear to pieces the skin of whoever was taking care of them. A mother's décolletage would be covered in cuts. But what was scariest of all was how the baby, in moving her hands and feet, could cut her own skin. Shiori wasn't moving them that much, but she could still reach her face.

It was a frightening business trimming those nails, like tiny grains of Swarovski crystal, or even tinier than that. She was using special nail scissors for babies, but the force you had to apply to these was in inverse proportion to their size.

"Oh, this is scary," Kaori groaned, which made Keisuke glance up from the notebook where he was writing something in pencil. He used little notebooks to jot down memos and sketches he came up with. He carried them about with him everywhere, and there were always a few dotted around the living room. Even little sketches and scribbles could become ideas for manga, so these were part of his bread and butter.

"Shall I trim them?"

Seriously? Three years of marriage and finally showing some initiative?

"Just do it as much as you can."

He did it bit by bit, and managed to do several fingers, making an excellent job of it at that. From that moment, he did a nail check every day.

Keisuke would take Shiori in his arms and settle down on the floor, legs crossed and nail scissors in hand.

"Don't cut her fingers, and don't trim them down too far."

"I'll be okay, I think."

The *I think* was a little scary, but he was quite proficient by this time. When her little balled fists opened, he'd quickly grab a hand and trim one or two fingers. When he was able to, he'd do three or four fingers at a time.

"Wow, you're really good."

"Like back when I used to paste tone film."

Manga artists had switched to digital now, but back in the analog age *Keisuke Tsukuda* was known for his beautiful tone work, in which thin pieces of film would be pasted onto a scene in a manga.

"Goodness, you're much better than me."

"At this kind of thing, yeah—and it's easier than with Spin."

Spin was on the sofa, flashing her furry belly.

"Kittens' nails are proper weapons, aren't they," Keisuke went on.

If a baby's nails were razors, then a kitten's were hooks. And they were thin, so they could really pierce. When a young cat's tendons had grown enough to allow it to extend and retract its claws, the muscle strength in its paws also developed and it could mercilessly stick them into anything, like hooks sinking in.

"I looked into it after Spin arrived. Cats' claws are curved, so if they leave them extended, they could dig into their own pads, right?"

"Yeah, if they keep them extended. Cats brought up indoors don't walk around enough for their nails to be naturally whittled down, and so some of them have terrible hangnails," said Kaori.

"It makes you cry just thinking about a cat's nails cutting into those cute, squishy little pink paws . . ."

"Would you focus now on those cute, squishy little pink *fingers* for me?"

"And with cats' nails, if you cut them too much, they'll bleed, won't they?" Keisuke mused. "They hate getting them cut, and struggle so much I'd be scared about hurting them."

"If Shiori gets hurt, I'm going to kill you."

"Compared to Spin, Shiori minds her manners. It's easy."

The cat first, eh? The cat's the boss after all.

Meanwhile, all the fingers and toes had been done, and Kaori declared Keisuke to be their official nail trimmer.

As she discovered, raising a cat helped them in many ways.

During the day, babies needed to be nursed every two or three hours, a relentless schedule that never let up. And the same held true in the middle of the night. Kaori would be in bed, having just fallen asleep, when that distinctive siren wail blasted out.

Her breast milk had dried up while she was still at her parents' house, and so she'd crawl out of bed to get *Milk! Milk!*

Kaori was just getting out of bed, when—

"I'll make it, you go back to sleep," murmured Keisuke.

She would have loved to, but the blaring milk siren was too

insistent to ignore, so she lifted Shiori out of the crib and stroked her forehead. She could hear a faint clatter from the kitchen downstairs as Keisuke bustled about.

Husbands never get up at night, a mother at her workplace at the publishing company had warned her. In other words, don't count on them to join the battle in the middle of the night. But until now, Keisuke had never once failed to attend to the baby siren.

"Because, you know—Spin," he said.

Again with the cat.

Spin, who'd been abandoned before she was weaned, had, in the space of two weeks, adjusted to drinking milk, he told her. Spin was on a two-hour timer, too, he added.

A kitten's siren was piercing, like a warning alarm on a machine, and it was impossible to sleep through it. Shiori's was much easier on the ears.

"If I don't take care of Spin, she'll die."

Kaori was amazed at how meticulously he carried out the operation of feeding Spin. He'd heat up milk, ensuring it was the right temperature, and before giving it to her, he'd wet her tiny bottom with a tissue dipped in warm water to stimulate her to poop. She could choke if he fed her when she was lying on her back, so he got her to crouch like a miniature Sphinx and fed her that way, not forgetting to sterilize the bottle afterward. Kaori was astonished at how perfectly he had mastered it.

Even at Kaori's parental home, where they'd never lived

without a cat, she'd not seen such sensitive caring for a kitten. And she had never done it herself; she'd always let her mother handle it.

There was no excuse for cutting corners. And this clearly helpless little ball of fur had changed Keisuke so much.

"You really did a good job, for *you*," Kaori commented.

Her comment implied a lot more, and Keisuke gave an embarrassed smile.

"These days, we've got Dr. Google and Master Yahoo to help us," he said.

Intrigued by his comment, Kaori opened the website history on the tablet they shared and marveled at how active Keisuke's private Yahoo account had been.

Question: I found an abandoned kitten. The vet said to use damp cotton wool to get her to pee, but I don't have any in the house. What should I do?

Answer: Tissues work just as well.

Answer: If there are any women in the house, wouldn't you have some makeup wipes? They sell them at convenience stores, you know.

Answer: Make sure you use warm water to wet the cotton wool or tissues! Cold water won't work and the kitten will catch a cold.

Question: Sorry to bother you again. The kitten-pee guy here. The kitten won't drink milk from the bottle. It will put the teat in its mouth but then turn away. What should I do?

Answer: Is the milk at the right temperature? It should be slightly warmer than a person's body temperature (38–40°C). Check the temperature on your wrist.

Answer: Is it too warm? Mix it with cooled-down hot water, shake the bottle and let it cool.

Question: Hot water that's been cooled down? What's that?

Answer: Google it, stupid!

Answer: It means water that's been boiled and left to cool. You boil it at about 70°C. Pour it into a baby-feeding bottle and cool it under cold running water.

Question: If the temperature for drinking is 40°C, can't you just heat it up in a microwave?

Answer: You boil it to get rid of the chlorine and chalk in the water, so do that and then cool it down.

Answer: Are you trying to kill the cat?

Answer: You could just set your electric hot-water dispenser to keep the water at 70°C. After it boils, it will keep it at that temperature.

Question: So it has that kind of convenient setting? I'll check it out!

Answer: Are you saying you've never used your hot-water dispenser?

Question: My wife's always taken care of things around the house . . . Right now she's back at her parents' place to have our baby. So until she gets back, I have to take care of the kitten by myself.

Answer: Whoa, that's some terrible wife, I'd say.

Answer: She wants you to do everything. Grounds for divorce.

Question: Really, grounds for divorce?

Answer: I'll see you in family court! From your wife.

Answer: I predict that you'll let the cat die before your wife gets home.

Question: I don't want it to die. So, which is better—to cool down the milk, or heat it up?

Answer: *You* have to decide, kitten-pee guy! How are we supposed to know what temperature your milk is?

Answer: Is this guy trolling?

Answer: Faster to just make up a new bottle. Stop posting—go and do it right now.

Answer: He's trolling. This cat does not exist.

Answer: If he's not trolling, this little cat is gonna die. That's why I'm responding—for the baby cat that *might* exist.

This led to a minor flurry of comments on the blog, an uproar about this may-or-may-not-actually-exist cat, with a few *screw you*–type responses mixed in. In the end, the class assembly decided he had to confess all this to his wife. My apologies, everyone, for being a hopeless husband.

Question: Sorry to keep bothering you. Cat Pee here . . .

Cat Pee finally became his online pseudonym.

> . . . Thank you so much for the advice about milk the other day. By the way, though she pees fine every day, I haven't seen anything that looks like poop. I wonder if she's sick?

Answer: Is she drinking all the milk? If she is, then I wouldn't worry about it. Kittens' poop is so thin, you're just not noticing it.

Answer: Golden Milk for little cats is nearly 100 percent absorbed by them, so while they're still on milk they sometimes don't poop.

Answer: When you wiped her butt to get her to poop, was there ever a thin yellow line? That's poop. But tell me, have you confessed to your wife?

Question: A thin yellow line! So that's poop! I haven't been able to say anything to my wife yet . . .

Answer: Hurry up and tell her. What'll you do if your wife gets angry and orders you to get rid of the cat?

Question: My wife isn't that kind of person. At least she
wouldn't make a kitten suffer, I know that.
Answer: Then why not tell her?

Question: I'm sure she'll blow her top . . .
Answer: They say people bring it on themselves.
Answer: Well, she might say to put the kitten in a foster
home.

Question: That would be hard . . . I can't imagine giving her up
after all this . . . She's coming back next week with
our child, and I think I'd prefer to let her know
first . . .
Answer: You're kind of a procrastinator, aren't you, when
things are tough.

They had no way of knowing how he'd once put things off
so much, he'd nearly been a tax evader.

Answer: I reckon he'll never ever tell her. I'm willing to bet a
million Zimbabwean dollars on it!

In the end everything had worked out, even if they'd bet
yen on it. After the million Zimbabwean dollars remark, there
were occasional responses on the thread, such as How's the cat's
pee now? and Wonder if he's in the family court?

..

Kaori heard footsteps hurrying up the stairs.

"Oh, that must be Spin, on her way!"

They put Spin in a cage in the living room at night, but Keisuke seemed to have let her out. Maybe he was planning to stay up and work. His deadline wasn't for a while, but he did have a one-shot manga assignment he had to complete.

Spin placed her front paws on Kaori's shin and dropped her head to sniff, seemingly concerned about what was taking place above her. She seemed to be worried about Shiori crying. During the day, too, if Shiori was nearby, Spin often padded inquisitively over. Shiori didn't show signs of reacting badly to the cat, so they were more often taking her out of the bouncer and letting her lie down on a baby futon on the floor, and when she was, Spin could be found snuggling up next to her, grooming her furry undercarriage, the picture of a harmonious twosome.

Because of all of you, we're getting along well, Kaori thought, silently thanking all those online respondents.

"Sorry to keep you waiting," Keisuke said, finally making an appearance, milk bottle in hand. The milk was at just the right temperature for the baby.

Kaori gave Shiori the teat and the siren came to an abrupt halt. She gurgled and cooed as she sucked down the milk.

"You see that, Spin? How Shiori's drinking her milk? What a good girl—"

His hands wrapped around her belly, Keisuke lifted Spin up,

and she must have smelled the milk since she extended her paws and scratched at the bottle.

"You've graduated from milk, right?"

Her teeth had grown in, strong enough to bite off a teat on a bottle. A cat's teeth came through much faster than a human's did.

"Are you going to do some work?"

"I'm wide awake now, so I reckoned why not."

Keisuke was basically a night owl to begin with. During Kaori's maternity leave this was helpful, as they could divide up the daytime and nighttime duties.

"I want to tweak the plot of my new work a bit. But it's kind of hard."

This was a touchy subject. Ever since his one big hit a few years ago, he'd had no long-running series. His other series were seen as okay pieces of work, but never went beyond more than a few volumes when they were published as separate books. The editorial department was hoping he'd come up with a new series that was even better, but the word online was that he'd never write anything to top that earlier hit, and Keisuke didn't have a strong enough will to avoid egosurfing the net—and telling a creative to not egosurf was ignoring human nature, plain and simple.

Creators were human beings, and human beings instinctively cared how others reacted to what they created. How many people in the world, when ordered to put a lid on that instinct, could actually comply?

The attitude of the editorial staff had changed substantially. In the past, they'd tell their authors not to worry about what was being said online, because if the authors did get to know, they'd either be inflated by praise or worn down by criticism. This was especially true of newcomers. Older hands weren't yet as affected. It was a different era now from the days when editors could conceal critical feedback from their authors.

Kaori's record in accounting surpassed what she'd done as an editor, but still she had once harbored ambitions as an editor.

"I love *Keisuke Tsukuda*'s manga," she'd said.

Even though it wasn't what had pushed her into marrying him, it's true she had said, "When *Keisuke Tsukuda*'s work comes out, I'll buy *Keisuke Tsukuda*'s work, no matter what the genre."

His earlier hit had been an action manga featuring characters with special powers. She had wanted to read whatever he wrote, be it a rom-com manga or one set in the workplace.

"Nor does it have to be science fiction, necessarily."

Kaori had also liked a serialization he'd done earlier, a teen rom-com story. He seemed to be able to pull off everyday, realistic manga as well.

"If you aim for a long-term serialization, it'll be obvious how you think you should stick to the genre you're especially good at . . . So it's best not to plan things out too much."

That wasn't what he was cut out for. He was the type who,

left to dig where he wanted, would eventually hit the mother lode.

As Shiori drained her bottle, the online chat room still lingered in Kaori's mind.

"Good girl—now give me a burp, a little burp."

Kaori jiggled her a bit and patted her back, and Keisuke picked up the bottle she'd put aside and got up to take it to the kitchen. The guy was well trained, she thought.

"I'm going to my study to work. Go back to sleep if you can."

As he toddled out of the room, another set of feet followed him. The drill instructor. The three weeks they'd spent together had been extremely bonding, and Spin gravitated much more toward Keisuke than to Kaori.

Kaori's drill instructor had been the midwife. For her mother this was her first grandchild, and it had been years since she'd had anything to do with babies, so she was relegated to assistant drill instructor. The head instructor, the midwife, had been the one who drummed the basic principles into Kaori's head.

One thing she'd told her was: whether it's using the bathroom, eating or making sure you're presentable, don't cut these activities short even if the baby is crying.

It was human nature for young mothers to want to rush to their baby's side as soon as it started crying, but as long as it's crying it's alive, the midwife had taught her, so prioritize your own needs, including use of the bathroom, making sure to eat and keeping yourself clean and presentable.

When a baby was really in trouble it wouldn't cry, but fall silently into a life-threatening situation.

Talk about frightening!

Even with crying, there were very different types.

There was your ordinary, business-as-usual crying and the declaring-a-state-of-emergency crying, and a mother needed to be able to distinguish between the two. No one else takes care of a mother's need to use the bathroom or eat or look after herself. You have to listen attentively to your baby's crying while you're using the toilet, eating, applying a little lipstick.

Seriously?

Making yourself presentable couldn't be so important, could it? was Kaori's thought, but a mother's emotional health was vital.

And more than that—

If you were just wearing any old thing and suddenly had a visitor and couldn't greet him or her, that would be a problem. In other words, she should make sure she looked neat enough to at least go to the door if there was a mail delivery.

Even with her husband with his lack of social skills added to the mix, by the time she left her parents' home, Kaori had accrued enough experience to prevent her baby from being in danger, and things were less stressful than she'd thought.

And much of the credit for this had to go to their wonderful drill instructor, Spin.

Spin, who'd grown up at a rate that far outstripped that of her little human companion, had reached the point where she was coordinated enough to climb to the top of their net curtains. A skill they had hoped she wouldn't acquire. Going up was one thing, but she couldn't climb down and would hang there, upside down at the top, meowing. Not a *Help!* sort of meow but more of a desperate plea to *Get me down!*

"What's going to happen when she gets heavier?" Keisuke asked. "If her claws get caught, they'll rip out . . ."

"You really want to know?" Kaori laughed with a snort. "What'll happen is the curtain will tear."

At her parents' home, every time they got a new kitten, the curtains would soon be in tatters. Even the *fusuma* sliding doors got ripped.

"I wonder if we should put in blinds instead."

"They'll just snap off."

Interior furnishings were definitely not designed with cats in mind.

"Should I make some lunch?" Keisuke suggested. Kaori had been cradling the baby for nearly an hour.

"No, it's about time to put her down."

She was happy Keisuke was concerned about her, but he hadn't progressed beyond the kind of cuisine that required just pouring in hot water and waiting three minutes. Kaori herself wasn't exactly a great cook, but she always kept some frozen udon noodles in the freezer. She figured she'd zap them in the microwave, and make kamatama udon with a raw egg and soy sauce and, to really liven it up, add some chopped spring onions.

When it was ready she'd add some crushed nori or ground sesame seeds, or even a little grated cheese to give a richer, Western taste. Wait—if she wanted richer, she could put in *tenkasu*, the crunchy bits of dough from tempura, she thought.

Searching for the point of overlap between what was quick and what she wanted to eat, she steeled herself and lowered Shiori onto the bed. The moment the baby's back had actually touched the futon, her eyes popped wide open and she showed an *Et tu, Brute?* look she'd been saving up and let out a lusty war cry.

"If she's crying, that means she's alive."

"If she's crying, that means she's not dead."

They voiced these watchwords to buck each other up.

And just then Spin padded over. They expected she might try to groom Shiori's hair, but instead she pressed her cheek into Shiori's side. Shiori let out a little cooing sound they hadn't heard before.

Spin began gently kneading Shirori's tummy with her paws, making the adults call out, *"Whoa! Wow!"*

They pulled out their mobile phones and began snapping rapid-fire shots. After several dozen clicks, they realized something: "No—we should *video* this!" and switched over.

They suddenly noticed Shiori's war cries had ceased. Her eyelids were drooping and finally they closed.

"*Seriously?*" they murmured simultaneously.

Spin's little pats finally slowed down and she herself went to sleep.

Fully savoring the afterglow, Kaori quietly got to her feet and made her way stealthily to the kitchen.

She zapped the noodles in the microwave, added a raw egg and soy sauce, chopped up some spring onions and shook in a good amount of grated cheese, with a final flourish of freshly ground pepper. She mixed these late-afternoon carbonara-style udon noodles with her chopsticks and she and Keisuke began slurping them up.

The dish would never make it onto a café menu but was excellent for a busy couple juggling two small creatures.

After that they often observed Spin's little baby-soothing pats. When Spin kneaded lightly on Shiori's side, it never failed to put her straight to sleep. Figuring that lightly patting their baby's side was the switch to get her to sleep, the adults began to imitate Spin with their fingertips, but only Spin could make it work. Perhaps because they couldn't reproduce the advanced pitter-patter movements that Spin had down to a T, or maybe it was because they were too caught up in a desire to rush their baby and make her *go to sleep!*

While Shiori was sleeping, it was the ideal time for cleaning the house. As Kaori pushed the floor wiper around on the first floor, she heard footsteps tramping up the stairs.

Don't wake Shiori! she thought, and a head-on collision of scolding was just about to happen when Keisuke called out, "Kaori, what should I do?!"

"About *what*?"

"This!"

He held out the tablet. The screen displayed the "Yahoo! Japan" app.

What really startled her was how many sketches he'd posted, all executed in a style she knew so well, of a sleeping baby and a kitten.

"What have you done?" she wanted to yell, but with no time for fury, she scrolled down the thread.

Question: Thank you so *much*, everyone, for your help the other day. Thanks to you all, the kitten has become a real member of our family. And she gets along with our baby so well, too. As a thank-you, I've uploaded a few sketches.

Answer: Wow, they're great!

Answer: I'm glad everything worked out. The drawings are amazing!

Answer: I'm guessing these aren't the work of an amateur . . .

Answer: Are you a pro? An illustrator? A manga artist?

Answer: Thanking us with sketches—now that takes some confidence. It's possible he *is* a pro.

Answer: Already married, with a new baby, a man . . . so not someone doing *shojo* manga . . .

The thread bounced around guesses about his identity.
Oh no! No, no, no!

A quick scan showed nobody had brought up the name Keisuke Tsukuda. They were quick, rough sketches, so it was hard to pinpoint the artist. Thankfully, too, there were no social networking sites with the name *Keisuke Tsukuda*. If he had been regularly posting drawings online, then that might have given away his identity.

"A few sketches to thank you? Are you kidding me?"

Kaori almost whacked him on the head.

"I just wanted to thank them, that's all . . ."

"You've got to understand you're much, much better than just anyone. At least at drawing!"

"What should I do? Delete them? My name hasn't come up yet."

To delete or not to delete? This was the crucial question when it came to keeping it from blowing up. *They're by someone else, make it someone else. Decide calmly, like you're an uninvolved third party.*

"I think it's best not to delete."

Suppressing the fear that seemed to be welling up, that he'd be recognized, he managed to wring out this decision. Delete them and it was very possible this would prod people to correctly identify him. But even if the name *Keisuke Tsukuda* did come up, it would just be mentioned in passing as one of many possible candidates.

"Don't ever enter this thread again. From now on, SNSs are strictly off-limits."

"Okay, I won't touch them. Too scary."

With his lack of social skills and general pessimism, what he feared more than anything was a back-and-forth online with other manga artists. In some areas, he was very conscious that his inability to read the room might lead to a sticky situation. His own SNS accounts were all under his personalized name K@rom and locked, and besides, he hadn't posted on them at all.

When Kaori had finished cleaning, she came downstairs and found Keisuke fast asleep, curled up like a bug next to Shiori on her futon, probably worn-out by the fear that he would be outed.

The source of all this must be the notebook in the living room, she thought, and went to fetch it. The pictures in question must be toward the back of the notebook.

Goodness, he's become a real parent now, hasn't he.

Kaori's eyes started to get itchy. No, it was more a feeling in her chest.

It was Shiori and Spin all over the place. Drawings of them covered the pages of the notebook, which was about to run out of space.

Out of the corner of her eye she spied an orange furball

coming toward her. Spin then curved her back upward in an elegant stretch. Every time she needed a stretch, she would come over where they could see her.

Kaori snapped her fingers to beckon her over, and Spin responded, skipping toward her, happy tail trembling.

"It's all thanks to you," Kaori said.

Because it was Keisuke who'd gone to take out the rubbish that day, this tiny Schrödinger's Kitten made itself observed. What a happy Uncertainty Principle it had turned out to be.

Kaori took a felt-tip pen from the stand on the table. She wrote *Excellent!* under the final sketch in the notebook. And added: *What's not to love!*

A sudden thought came to her—it was in ink so it was there to stay. *Don't get me wrong*, she thought—*I'm evaluating the drawing, not* you.

She closed the notebook and left it where she found it. When she opened it again a few days later, it was full of new sketches. Fearing she might see something scary, she turned back to the spot where she'd added her comments. There Keisuke had shyly added a self-portrait and the words *Me too.* Wait a second—this had been her comment on the drawing, not on him.

Kaori would occasionally jot down some notes when she saw Shiori and Spin together. Kind of like an exchange of diaries. A few days would pass, and she'd see how Keisuke had taken an idea from her memo, one easily drawn, and made a one-panel comic out of it.

How does her tail stick up exactly?

Sometimes she'd check the details.

So cute, so very, very cute. Adorable. Cute and adorable, adorable, adorable.

A lovefest filling page after page. A new notebook began, and from the first page it was a flood of love.

Shiori's weight had doubled now. She'd graduated from infant diapers to size S. She could support her head by herself. And she could laugh. When her poop leaked out from the diaper, it was like the end of the world and she'd wail. *She can see well now, right? The way her eyes follow Spin. Today she looked Kaori in the eye and could see her!*

As predicted, the net curtain got ripped. Torn from top to bottom, three claws' worth. Spin started eating crunchy cat food. When her poop stuck to her backside, she'd race about in a panic, meowing her head off. She slept with Shiori's crotch as a pillow. *The diaper is a cushion? Doesn't it smell?*

Not every day was a good day. There were times when Keisuke felt down in the dumps or under pressure. He and Kaori quarreled occasionally over what was best for their baby, and for their cat. But he only put things in the notebook they could laugh over someday.

They filled the notebook only with items that, if Shiori were to see them later, would show their love for her.

Keisuke had a break from the short-term serialized manga he'd been working on. He was now planning a new work. Kaori was busy gathering information on childcare, kindergarten hunting.

When she was less than a year old, Spin was neutered. When she came home after the operation, her expression was one of betrayal. *You humans. I'm never going to trust you ever again.* About an hour later, she was rolling and rubbing herself against them like always. "Who could have done such a horrible thing to our little Spin," Kaori cooed over and over, doing her best to offer comfort.

Shiori started to crawl and had to be watched even more closely. The words of an experienced mother friend hit home: "Wait until they start to move around. That's when the 'fun' really begins." Every five minutes brought a new way of dying by suicide. Even a plastic spoon could be lethal for a small human with a death wish.

In the midst of all this, Keisuke came to her one day, a serious look on his face. "I have something I need to ask you," he said. "My editor asked me if I'd write something for *Healthy Child*."

This was a high-profile magazine for bringing up babies, published by Kaori's company.

When he'd gone to the editorial offices to talk about a new manga series and was asked what theme he was interested in these days, Keisuke had said, "Well, if it's about kids and cats, I've got a ton of material." He'd said it as a joke, but his editor took him at his word, the upshot being a commission for *Healthy Child*.

Comic essays about a husband who enjoys spending time with his own child? He and Kaori laughed uproariously at the idea.

"Hmm," said Keisuke. "I guess that wouldn't work, would it?"

"Well—it might."

She found it funny to think of Keisuke as one of those gung ho fathers, a man who fully engaged in the real world.

"Why not give it a try? The material you have in your notebooks is great."

At some point, he'd moved from just sketches to framing the drawings like manga, and she was thinking it was a waste not to share these with the world.

"I think a kind of full-blown comic essay could be really popular."

They settled on *The Schrödinger Daddy* as the series title.

Hello. My name's Keisuke Tsukuda. I usually write sci-fi action manga . . . went the intro for the opening piece.

Schrödinger's law stated that until you observed the cat inside the box, you couldn't know if it was alive or dead, in the same way that Kaori wouldn't know if her husband would pass or fail as a new father until she tried opening the box. His wife, before she observed anything, was sure he'd fail.

He wrote about it all—how when she found out she was

pregnant, they squabbled to the point where divorce seemed imminent; how he worried that even when he saw his baby's face, he still wouldn't have any fatherly feeling—the first episode ending as he rescued a still-unweaned kitten. And readers lapped it up, a survey later ranking this first episode the most popular story in the magazine.

Everyone, I really want to thank you for helping me, he wrote—and the "Yahoo! Japan" thread buzzed to life again with posts such as I never imagined it was Keisuke Tsukuda!

Concerned that he wasn't so well known to readers of a magazine aimed at parents of young children, he opened each episode with the same *I usually write sci-fi action manga* introduction until finally Editorial updated the byline to *An essay by a manga artist who also writes sci-fi action manga.*

He was the type of manga artist who beavered away at whatever he fancied until he happened to strike a rich vein of ore, and though this time the vein he'd unearthed wasn't a major hit, it did look like it might have a long shelf life. He'd always had an eye for the magic of the everyday.

Its popularity led to cat-related manga drawings, and unusually he and Spin were featured in a TV report about the relationship between a manga artist and his cat. The production team were eager to include his baby daughter and wife, but Keisuke turned them down with a firm *No*.

Instead, they concentrated on his other work, and so his earlier books began to shift more copies.

"Spin-chan, you've been our lucky *maneki-neko*, haven't you now, you liddle cutie . . ." Keisuke said in an embarrassing baby-like voice, giving firm strokes along her back, until he ended up with a claws-in cat-punch to the side of his head.

"Daddy's such a liddle dummy now, isn't he . . ." Kaori said to Shiori.

Kaori herself had become completely inured to this kind of baby talk. Baby Shiori, though, shot her a look of disgust.

"That's how babies talk, Mommy," she said.

Sometimes Kaori wondered what would have happened if Keisuke hadn't rescued Spin that day.

The inside of the Mikkabi tangerine box. What was observed was a live cat whose sibling had just passed away. Perhaps also notable was what would happen to the very observer whose life was touched by that very cat.

Good Father / Bad Father

Dad was never that fond of cats to begin with.

Even when pressure came from the kids to get a cat, and they found one advertised in the *Free Giveaways* newspaper under the "Kittens Available" section, still Dad didn't show much interest.

The pale brown kitten that arrived was a male, advertised as just two months old, but must have been three times older than that.

The man who dropped off the kitten by car said his hobby was fishing, and just as he was leaving, he bent over the kitten and said, "Next time I'll bring over a fish I caught for you," though he never showed up again. As an aside, the man spoke the local dialect, which tacked on a *nyaa* or a *chuu* to the end of each word, and was mocked for sounding like "a cat and a mouse having a conversation."

According to the man, the kitten had been living with another family for a while, but they gave him back, which might explain the kitten's slightly sulky vibe. After the man left, the kitten lay down on the floor beside the sliding glass doors in the living room, a nice sunny spot, with a *Well, I'm only here temporarily* look.

He didn't try to scratch you or anything, but he certainly didn't seem to go out of his way to ingratiate himself with his new family, and the kids, who'd been looking forward to getting a cute kitten, were frankly disappointed. Mom, who had dealt with the kitten's owner when he first came by, was, she admitted, hesitant about taking him initially.

"I thought he seemed pretty damn big for two months," she said.

Mom was a timid person and perhaps couldn't bring herself to say to the kitten's owner, "Thanks for bringing him over, but he's too big and we don't need him."

"It's a little unfair on your father," she said.

No one in the family found this past-his-prime kitten very appealing. Dad, though, was the most outspoken of all.

He had given the kitten a long look, listened as Mom explained the background, before coming out with:

"The first family must have sent him back because of his looks."

Everyone was thinking the same but didn't dare say so. At the time there was a popular male singer with a smooth voice who appeared on TV a lot, and when Dad saw him, he'd said, *This guy certainly isn't getting by on his looks, that's for sure.* In typical Dad fashion, he was trying to say that the guy was a very good singer.

"I bet the guy who dropped off the kitten thought, *Good riddance.*" He seemed to find it amusing, perhaps picturing to himself the old guy sighing in relief as he walked out the door.

"If we give back this kitten, I doubt he'll be able to find anyone else to take him."

In his roundabout way, Dad was telling them to keep him. So the pale brown cat became a member of the family, and with his tiger stripes they named him, simply, Tora—*Tiger*.

Mom and the kids had been thinking that if they were getting a kitten, they should have at least got a cuter, more lovable one, but Dad was totally unconcerned. This was a man who, after all, didn't care much about animals. A guy who, when asked what was his favorite animal, replied, *A hyena*. Not exactly what most people would say. Ask him what he liked about hyenas and he'd answer, *They keep low to the ground.*

"We could learn a lot from them. Hyenas don't stay low like that because it's in their nature, but because of their skeletal structure. I like the spotted hyenas better than the striped ones. Because they're more seedy looking and melancholy," he added.

Most people would lump striped and spotted hyenas together. But not Dad, who often went to a zoo in the next prefecture, where they had both. This was, typically, just a passing fad on his part, and didn't mean he was becoming soft on animals. He was the type who, when he found something interesting, would obsess about it for a while, but the obsession never lasted. He was good at discovering little hobbies for himself like that.

The construction company where he worked was involved in the massive Seto Bridge project, building a link between

Okayama and the island of Shikoku, and just before the bridge was completed, he became totally obsessive about it, collecting posters and picture postcards of it, and without first obtaining permission, signed up his whole family for a special daylong bus tour that would allow them to walk across the bridge before it opened for business. They hadn't heard a thing about it until one morning when he woke them all up at the crack of dawn to board the bus. Since it was a tour, they couldn't very well give up and go home halfway through, so they had to march like troopers along the dark and shining asphalt of the bridge.

When they asked which part of the bridge Dad's company had been involved in building, it turned out to be the stretch that connected the bridge to the road. His company had somehow wormed its way into building a small part of this massive public works project in another prefecture. Come to think of it, his company must have been a pretty ambitious firm to land that kind of contract, however small.

Besides Dad, there were plenty of other parents rash enough—since final checks were still to be made—to bring their families along on the tour, and so there were a lot of visitors walking about on the bridge, literally as far as the eye could see. On the way back, almost everyone fell asleep, but one girl was woken up by the swaying of the bus and saw that, for some reason, the TV was showing *The Story of Hachi-ko*, a film about the famous dog also remembered in the form of a bronze statue in Tokyo. She had no idea what happened to the dog or its master, because she dropped off again shortly afterward and by the time she woke up, the credits were rolling.

But this story is about a cat, not a dog.

Most people at the time kept their dogs outside and let their cats roam wherever they wanted, and so, in line with tradition, Tora had a pretty random upbringing. When he reached puberty and was neutered, there was no cat carrier in the house, so he was placed in a cardboard box, which was then wedged into the pannier basket on Mom's little motor scooter, and off they went to the vet's. Naturally any cat suddenly finding itself shut up in a box would panic, and Tora struggled so mightily it made it hard for Mom to steer. Finally, Tora managed to thrust a paw between the cardboard flaps at the top of the box, and with the vet's only one traffic light away, it looked as if he was about to escape. They'd underestimated their cat's athletic ability.

Dad had said: "A box is perfectly good for a cat. Plus the vet's not so far away, so it's a waste of money to buy a carrier." But Mom had had enough, so by the time Tora was discharged from the vet's, she'd already ordered a carrier from the nearest DIY store.

"Hard to believe you made it all the way here," the vet had told her, a bit stunned at the sight of the box, and his comment had obviously got to her.

"Dad was so stingy, it made me so embarrassed," she said when she got back home, clearly upset. "And if Tora-chan had ripped open the box and escaped, he might very well have been hit by a car and badly hurt."

"Okay, okay, but he came out of it all right, didn't he? So all's well that ends well."

If all this had happened now, Dad would have been roundly abused by one of those animal rights groups. And it wasn't as if he didn't like Tora or anything.

"He had those cute little plump balls before," Dad said, poking and prodding at Tora's deflated little scrotum. He moved Tora's thick, crooked tail around like a gear lever: "Look, he's changing gears." Tora gave him a look but just let him carry on. The cat wasn't exactly very friendly, but you had to admit he was pretty tolerant.

Once, Tora had been put inside a carrier bag hanging from a hook on the back of a door. It wasn't the kids who had put him there, but Dad.

"He'd stuck his face inside the bag, and seemed to be sniffing around, and when I gave him a little push so that he ended up inside the bag, he seemed surprisingly okay about it, so I hung the bag from the hook."

Until the moment Mom found him and let him out, he hadn't made a peep, and had curled up inside the bag. Hard to tell if he was just being stoical or whether he actually liked it in there. When she put him down, he unhurriedly sauntered off, his tail quivering as he went.

This unfriendly, long-suffering cat lived with them for eighteen years. The children had all grown up and flown the nest by then, and though Tora had always niftily made himself at home wherever he pleased, now he had all of a sudden become quite weak.

He had always been a nonchalant cat and his back legs, even from the outset, were never that sturdy. But they now became seriously unsteady, his knees so feeble he'd have to rest after each step on his way upstairs.

He got to the point where he couldn't even step over the side of the litter tray, and often soiled the floor. They got rid of the litter tray and spread plastic sheets on the floor, but he seemed at a loss for what to do and tended to find somewhere else to relieve himself. Usually on the carpet or the futon cushions. Cleaning up after him became too laborious, so they made diapers for him. In those days, pet diapers didn't exist, so Mom cut a hole for his tail in a baby's diaper and put it on him.

When it looked like he was not long for this world, the children were contacted by phone. The eldest daughter lived far away and only came by when she had time off, so it was the cool, detached daughter number two who stopped by their house regularly.

When Dad came home in the evenings, he'd look at Tora and say, "You still alive and kicking?" Mom scolded him for his lack of delicacy, but that's the way he was.

The eldest daughter was at college in the Kansai region when the huge earthquake hit the area in 1995. She'd taken refuge in a park, and when the shaking finally ceased and she had got back home, the first thing she did was phone Mom and Dad. Never having experienced such violent shaking before, she was convinced all of Japan was about to get swallowed up.

It was just a little past six a.m. Still half-asleep, Mom answered the phone and, clearly a touch irritated, asked what was wrong. The daughter wanted to know if they'd got through the earthquake unscathed, but Mom hadn't realized anything was wrong. Finally convinced Japan hadn't been engulfed yet, the daughter hung up.

Immediately after their phone call, the phone lines to Kansai were cut off.

"She's pretty smart," Dad said, praising his eldest daughter for calling so quickly. Terrible scenes of the aftermath began to appear on TV, and when they tried to call their daughter back, they couldn't get through.

She's pretty smart—what kind of remark is that? their daughter had thought at the time. She knew that even when it came to well-meaning praise, Dad always came at things in a left-field way. Normal parents would probably have said something like, *Our daughter always has her act together.*

After the earthquake, when the phone lines were restored, Dad said to her, "Sure, you went through a lot, but you got through it, and now you have quite a story to tell." She'd thought that herself, though she didn't say it, nor did she think it was the kind of thing any dad would say to his daughter when she was stuck in lodgings without a proper flushing toilet, where fear of aftershocks meant she went to bed with her shoes on. The younger daughter summed it up neatly: "The man's got no heart."

Tora, in a diaper, spent the night in Mom's arms, and just before dawn, he passed away, peaceful to the end.

When he heard that Tora was gone, the dad with no heart simply nodded and said, "Oh, really?" It was as if he meant to say, *Well, he lived a good life.* Or maybe not.

This was a dad who liked hyenas. And so Tora's death did not affect him, not one bit.

M om was the one who suffered what people now call *pet loss.* The kids had pestered her for a cat, and she had been the one to look after him.

So while the loss of Tora had no effect on Dad, he did notice, in his own way, that Mom was seriously upset. He'd happened to reach mandatory retirement age and had begun to work at a part-time job that let him come and go as he pleased, and so he often took Mom on a drive for a change of scene. He had always loved car trips and would spend time looking for places to take her.

On this particular day, they were on their way to scoop up jellyfish from the ocean. A while back, the local post office and other shops that retailed local products had been selling special packs that enabled you to raise and observe jellyfish in your own home. Order one and you'd get a plastic fish tank with an actual living jellyfish inside it. According to their advertising, if you refilled it with fresh seawater, the jellyfish would live for a while, and when it began to weaken, you could return it to the sea. The pack came with a container of seawater to freshen the tank. It was a pretty shoddy product, if you think about it.

When jellyfish weaken, and can no longer swim, they turn a bluish black. Manufacturers of the packs expected that at this point you'd return the jellyfish to the sea, but Dad preferred to see it through to the bitter end.

"Why don't you take it back to the sea?" Mom urged him, but he ignored her. So the jellyfish met its end, floating life-lessly in the corner of the fish tank. Such a cruel way to go.

Even after this short-lived craze for keeping jellyfish blew over, Dad didn't give up on his hobby.

"You don't need to buy anything," he insisted. "There are tons of jellyfish we can scoop up inside the breakwater."

And so off he'd go with a net to drag the sea for glossy little jellyfish.

He soon realized it wouldn't do to catch anything that was too big. The fish tank being small and the oxygen insufficient, a large jellyfish would soon keel over.

"They've come up with a really nasty product." Mom sighed. "It was the same with the silkworms." This was when the kids were still in elementary school, where they were raising silk-worms to try to get them to spin a silk fan.

The school had purchased a silkworm pack that came with mulberry leaves for the caterpillars. When they reached the terminal larval stage, the caterpillars could be placed on the ribs of a fan, where they were supposed to spit out enough silk thread to create a fan. Whoever had come up with this system was clearly not firing on all cylinders.

Placed on top of the fan's ribs, the silkworms were driven to produce cocoons, but because the ribs of the fan were flat, there was no way the caterpillars could manage it, and so they'd try all sorts of methods of spitting up their thread, until they ended up crucified on top of the ribs of the fan.

"This is pretty awful," Dad had muttered, but without offering any help, so that Mom was left to cut the threads and rescue them. Later, she prepared a small cocooning frame in a box so they could spin their cocoons there.

Hard to tell what the difference was for him—why he'd expressed compassion for the silkworms but none for the jellyfish. This being the case, Mom had decided it was best to go along with him on his trips to scoop up jellyfish.

On one particular day, they were on a road that cut right across some fields when the line of cars in front started to slow down. They seemed to be making a detour around something.

"What's going on?" Dad said, peering ahead uncertainly, but it was Mom who spotted it first.

"Honey, it's a cat!"

Barely the size of a fist, a tiny kitten had crawled out from the grove beside the road and the cars ahead had been swerving widely to avoid it.

Mom figured Dad was about to swerve, too, but instead he pulled over onto the verge, just inches away from where the little cat sat mewling and waving its tail.

He put the handbrake on and got out.

Pyaoww! Pyaoww! went the cat, like a wailing siren. It was a light tortoiseshell mixed with patches of cream.

Mom, wanting to help it back into the bushes for its own safety, pushed it gently back toward the grove, but the kitten could not be persuaded and crawled straight back onto the road, and after several pushes, it reemerged every time.

"Maybe we should take it home with us."

What?

Mom couldn't believe her ears. Here they were, on the way to massacre some jellyfish. And now?

After watching Tora pass away, Mom had decided she didn't want another cat. She just didn't have the strength to say goodbye in that way ever again.

But once the decision had been made to take the kitten home, the tiny creature clung to Mom's hand with all its might.

"We still have Tora's litter tray, too," said Dad.

Getting rid of all their cat-related paraphernalia would have meant erasing all traces of Tora, which they couldn't bring themselves to do.

So that day they put a hold on the jellyfish massacres, and the kitten came home with them.

The kitten was a veritable paradise for fleas—you could spot them scampering around in its whisker pads—so the vet prescribed a strong anti-flea treatment. The kitten turned out to be female, and her eyes were only just opening. Nevertheless, during her examination by the vet, she protested loudly, her claws out.

The second-eldest daughter, who lived nearby, came over straightaway, her toddler in tow.

"You have to give her a name. What about *Ten*—Sky or Heaven? Wouldn't that be cute?"

It had very nearly been her daughter's name, though they hadn't ended up choosing it. It didn't sound good alongside her married surname.

With no suggestions from anyone else, *Ten* became the cat's name.

She ate voraciously and soon had chewed off the teat of the baby's bottle. Later, she started to chow down proper canned cat food. *Now you're talking! Why'd you all wait so long to give me this?* she seemed to be saying.

Their eldest daughter, who after studying in Kansai now lived in another prefecture, left her husband home by himself just to come over to cuddle the kitten.

"And you hardly ever come to visit," her father told her.

"Well, kittens are only a limited-time offer, so you've got to catch them while you can."

For all that, the main topic of conversation in their house was Dad. They each wondered what had got into him. They all had their own theories about what had made him take home a stray.

"Maybe he really did love Tora after all."

"Mmm. Don't think so. The day he died, all Dad said was, *Oh, really?*"

"And with all his killing of jellyfish, ceaselessly and ruthlessly."

Mom's wish had been simply that he'd stop with the jellyfish slaughter, and a cat, of all things, had turned out to be the answer to her prayers.

When his jellyfish obsession had finally subsided, they'd left the empty fish tank in a corner of the living room, and Ten would climb inside, in raptures, purring and mewling. For a cat, the dry, empty fish tank was simply a transparent box.

"Dad seems to like Ten a lot."

Whenever Ten clambered into the fish tank, Dad never said a thing. It seemed he'd given up enslaving jellyfish and no longer had any use for it.

Ten eventually grew tired of the fish tank and it was disposed of. Dad didn't complain then, either.

It was their son who came up with an answer of sorts to solve the puzzle about Dad's unpredictable behavior.

"Mom's been looking pretty drawn—maybe a new cat will perk her up?"

Apparently, Dad had muttered this to his son a while back, but with no intention of actually getting a cat, so when a kitten crawled in front of the car, it had been a genuine godsend.

For some strange reason, the kitten, at the height of her cute period, was very attached to Dad, and would rub up against his legs whenever he got up. Dad never did anything to look after the cat. He found all that touchy-feely business annoying and would lightly kick her aside, so the cat's devotion to him was hard to fathom.

All that kittenish attention did actually move this man

with no heart, this lover of hyenas (especially the spotted variety). He even started to buy toys for it.

Ten was still at the stage where she loved to play with toys, so every time Dad went out, he'd come home with something new. There were a couple of toys Ten showed no interest in, and Dad seemed to enjoy trying to figure out why certain toys weren't in favor. He got heavily into rifling through the hundred-yen shops to find something that would capture the kitten's fickle attention. He'd often come home with carrier bags bursting with absurd little items, and Mom found the whole thing quite a pain.

∽

Dad had always loved going out on car trips, but he finally reached an age where he had to give up driving, and so, against his will, he got rid of the car.

"I must be getting old. I'll be driving along and suddenly find there's too much space between me and the car in front."

He came out with this statement a few years earlier, when grazing the side of the car was becoming an everyday occurrence, as was shaving off parts of other people's walls.

"If you ever hit somebody, you won't recover from it," the son told him, almost forcibly taking the car from him and selling it.

Now without a car, he aged overnight. His wasn't the type of sunny personality who would make do with the bus or train, and since he didn't go out anymore, he started to lounge around the house in his pajamas, his legs getting visibly wobbly and his back weaker. The only old people who were as bent over and stooped as he was were the old grandpas from old-time fairy-tale manga.

The second-eldest daughter, who had a tendency to be snide, said he reminded her of a hairpin, which had Mom in stitches. That was a bit over the top, but he was so bent over, it made you wonder if he wasn't turning into a hunchback.

Nor was Dad the type to listen to any advice about getting exercise. The son, who'd quarreled quite a bit with him after he'd taken away the car, commented, "As long as he doesn't kill anyone, we should let him do what he wants."

Since Dad had enjoyed jellyfish so much, Mom kept suggesting that they take him to the jellyfish aquarium in Yamagata before he became completely immobile, and so the eldest daughter and her husband took on the task of arranging the outing.

As there was no direct flight to Yamagata from their area, they stayed at their daughter's place in Kansai, from which they would set off on their trip the following day.

When their daughter came to greet them at the arrivals gate, she had to wait what felt like hours for them to appear. The rest of the passengers had long since deplaned, but there was still no sign of Mom and Dad.

When, finally, they hobbled into view, she almost didn't recognize them.

"I thought it was an invalid and his carer."

Dad's burning interest in jellyfish seemed to have faded long ago, and so he wasn't all that keen to visit the aquarium. In fact, the trip was a total failure, Dad being his usual willful self.

Meanwhile, Ten was growing up. The wildcat side she'd first displayed on her visit to the vet's only strengthened, and soon it was impossible to get her into the carrier, as she was too big.

"If Ten gets sick," Mom said, "I'll do my best for her at home, but that's really all I can do."

The last time she'd taken Ten to the vet's had been a few years earlier, and according to her, the vet was clearly none too happy to see the cat. The vet and her staff never got through a visit from Ten without a bit of bloodshed.

Looking back on it, Tora now seemed an accomplished, gentle cat, and their nostalgia for him only increased.

Ten had grown up among butterflies and flowers, so how did she end up such a ferocious character? When their eldest daughter, the one who lived in another prefecture, came home on a rare visit, she'd flash her claws at her as she passed. She'd leap on her, too, when the daughter was napping on the sofa, aiming for her windpipe, clearly out for the kill.

Mom could not just stand by and watch, so she gave her daughter a can of luxury cat food.

"She cannot resist it, so give it a go," she said. But Ten wouldn't come near, watching from a safe distance with her eyes half-closed. *No way am I going to touch anything* you *give me*, she seemed to be saying to the daughter.

"Animals are a good judge of people" was Dad's smug remark, as Ten continued, as always, to be his fan alone.

When it got to the point where going upstairs was too much, they moved Dad's bed down to the Buddhist altar room just off the living room, and this space became his lair. And except for coming to the dining table or going to the toilet, he was like a bagworm, ensconced in his cocoon. As soon as Dad woke up, Ten would leap out from wherever she had chosen to rest, and coil around his legs as he tottered about. Dad went on lightly kicking her aside, but Ten's devotion showed no signs of abating.

"This cat is no judge of people," their daughter said angrily—clearly a case of sour grapes. "The only good thing about her is her face."

And it was true, she was a beautiful-looking cat. Irresistibly cute from the time she was a kitten.

"Maybe she remembers it was Dad who brought her back home. She *is* pretty intelligent," she said.

Being wary, too, was a sign of intelligence, according to her.

The eldest daughter, never having conquered her discomfort around Ten, finally got a cat of her own. A different breed, with a different face from Ten's, but hers, too, was quite the looker.

"My cat's cute, too, Dad," she said, opening the photos on her smartphone to show him, but he only snorted.

"Every cat in the world is cute," he shot back.

What did you say? The whole family was stunned. "Where's our dad, and what have you done with him?" Even in a worst-case scenario, Dad wasn't the type to say something so indulgent about cats. Despite what he said, when Ten got in his way he'd still give her a little kick.

Tottering along, rubbing up against him. Totter, totter, rub, rub. As if this scenario of old man and devoted cat would go on for a hundred years or more.

D ad's upbringing had led him to be a drinker, and he'd been a heavy smoker, too. He'd been told either cirrhosis of the liver or lung cancer would get him. In the end, it was both.

At one point, he seemed to cut back on his drinking, and though he always coughed when he inhaled on a cigarette, he didn't appear unwell. He was kind of holding his own against the passage of time, and his family took this as part of the aging process.

What was a far bigger problem for them was how his legs were giving way. Until one day he took to his bed, refused to get up and was hospitalized.

Humored by a lovely nurse, he did his rehabilitation and managed slowly to get back onto his feet and to totter around again. At the rehab center, they called it a miraculous resurrection.

The lovely nurse urged Dad to have a checkup, and that's

when they discovered the diseases. Both were terminal, and both inoperable. The doctors seemed amazed he was still alive.

Since there was nothing to be done, it seemed cruel to put Dad in a hospital again. Without giving him the details of his condition, they decided to take care of him at home in his final days.

He'd spent his life drinking incessantly, and smoking like a chimney, so it felt like it was all inevitable.

Mom took care of various end-of-life things for him. Just as she'd watched over their cat as it passed, she was full of generosity and kindness. And so he didn't seem to suffer much. Their son, a confirmed bachelor, came home to help.

Dad slept, and got up. Then he slept, slept, slept some more, then he got up. Spending his days in this routine, he began to grow a bit senile. "When's dinner?" he'd ask. "You already had it, Dad," came the answer. This kind of back-and-forth became a daily occurrence. The sensation of having eaten had perhaps deteriorated, because he often complained of being hungry.

Mom would hear sounds from the kitchen and, going to investigate, would find him rummaging through the drawers. He'd happily haul any sweets he'd discovered back to his bed, but the problem was that in among them were some of Ten's treats.

"Honey, those are Ten's snacks," Mom would say as she removed them. Often she'd make tea and they'd have a little nighttime drink while she bent over to give Ten the snacks Dad had accidentally pilfered.

Right up until the day he lost consciousness, Mom supported him when he went to the bathroom. Ten would wind herself around his unsteady legs as he walked, and Dad would, as usual, kick her away.

They thought he'd totter around forever, hanging in there, but once the pain took hold, it was the end of the road. He was the type who couldn't stand any pain or suffering, and had always avoided the dentist, even to the point where, by the time he turned sixty, he didn't have a tooth left in his head.

At some point during the marathon consumption of painkillers, he finally passed away. His eldest daughter and her husband hurried over, but arrived too late.

"He never did have any patience," she said.

They kept his body at home for two days, waiting for an opening at the crematorium, and he looked as though he was just sleeping. The room was maintained at a very low temperature with an air conditioner and dry ice, but everything else remained the same.

Dad had always hated formality, so they had a small private funeral. He was taken out of the altar room that had been his lair, and he came back to it again, this time as ashes.

While they were at the crematorium, the rental people came and took away the hospital bed. In its place, they set up a simple altar, where Mom placed his funerary tablet and an urn for his ashes.

Ten, who'd stayed at home all the while, turned up, unnoticed.

It was hard to tell if she understood what had happened, but she sat in the doorway staring for a time at the altar. Then she disappeared.

A year went by.

Their son, the confirmed bachelor, said he'd leave home after Dad died, but he ended up staying, and the three of them embarked on a new life together—Mom, son and cat.

Probably since her son was around, Mom didn't lose heart and stayed healthy.

Their son was always a quiet soul, so it was to her two daughters that she spoke the most. In a good mood, Mom said that when the weather improved, she wanted to see the Pallas's cat at Kobe Zoo. She'd heard about it some years before in an NHK documentary and was completely taken with it, being extremely curious about it before interest in the cat became a thing.

She'd clipped out newspaper articles about the cat and kept them under a table mat. If it hadn't been for Dad, she would have gone much earlier to see it, and stayed with their eldest daughter instead of at a hotel.

"That reminds me, how's Scary Cat doing?"

That was the daughter's name for Ten, who'd attacked her throat that time.

"She really does have a cute side to her, you know."

Mom always defended Ten, bragging about little things she did that, frankly, any cat would do.

"Now that you mention her . . ." Mom said. That day she had a new tidbit to share. Since it was winter, they kept the sliding glass doors between the altar room and the living room closed to keep the warm air from escaping. When Dad was alive, they'd left the doors open so it was essentially one big room.

"If we close the doors, Ten-chan starts to scratch, asking us to open them."

When they opened the sliding doors, Ten would pace around where Dad's bed had been and sit under the altar for a while, her tail wrapped around her body, her ears turned forward as if sensing something.

Even when left behind by him, the cat's devotion to the old man refused to fade.

"She was really close to Dad. Maybe Ten's the one who misses him the most?"

Dad's human family had accepted his passing, had cried soft tears at his funeral, yet they had made a quick recovery, knowing his time had come.

"But this cat really isn't a good judge of people. I mean, Dad never fed her, not even once."

"He didn't do a single thing to look after her. But Ten-chan really adored him."

Dad, who always did what he liked, whose words and manner were always so left-field, whose actions were often so preposterous that even other families noticed.

Whenever their daughters talked about Dad, their friends

would unfailingly chime in with: *If other people's dads do some-thing, it seems funny, but if your own dad does the same, you don't like it.*

But there was a cat who loved Dad unconditionally, so if you were to have the good-father/bad-father debate, this would be enough to push him over to the good-father side.

It wasn't that he even liked cats that much—he didn't—but in his later years, he had taken his family completely aback with his surprise comment, *Every cat in the world is cute.*

Merciless to jellyfish, merciful to cats. They could cancel each other out.

He was, when all was said and done, a good father. Trou-bled, troublesome, yet utterly adored by a lone cat who could love no one else.

No more to be said.

Cat Island

Ryo, why don't we go to Cat Island?"

We were eating dinner when my father, a freelance photographer, suddenly came out with this.

It was not long after my father had remarried following the death of my mother and we'd moved from Hokkaido to Okinawa.

Haruko, his new wife, was a lovely woman whose smile, like the sun, could light up a room. But I couldn't forget my real mother and couldn't bring myself to call Haruko *Mom*.

Looking back on it, it's hard for me to believe there ever was a time when I felt uncomfortable around her.

At the time, my father wanted me to get closer to Haruko, and at every opportunity would push us to *go out as a family*, which frankly got a little tiresome.

I was at a sensitive age then for a boy. The more he pushed me, the more I resisted the idea of calling Haruko *Mom*.

But the name *Cat Island* intrigued me. It sounded like the beginning of a fantasy adventure or something.

"What's Cat Island?" I asked Haruko, who was working as a tour guide. I was being considerate, drawing out her expertise, as a child will, at the dinner table.

"Its real name is Taketomijima," my father jumped in. "There are hundreds of cats there and there's been a bit of a buzz among cat lovers recently."

I had been trying to include Haruko, but my father, butting in with his usual adult thoughtlessness, torpedoed my efforts. My eyes met Haruko's, and we couldn't help but share a smile.

What a pain he can be, right?

I know.

"How do you get there?"

It was Haruko who responded to my question. Finally, my attempts to include her were paying off.

"You take a plane from Naha to Ishigakijima, then a high-speed boat that takes about ten minutes."

There are so many little islands in Okinawa, with lots of small planes hopping between them. I was finally getting a sense of the geography of the place, and how people could travel in small planes that buzzed back and forth between the islands.

"Katsu-san, so you accepted the job? To photograph the cats?" Haruko asked my father, who was holding out his empty teacup for a refill.

"Yeah. I couldn't say no," he replied, pulling a long face.

"Is that right?" Haruko said, tilting her head as she poured more tea into his cup.

"I told them I don't specialize in animal photography, but they said it would be okay."

Apparently an editorial staffer my father knew had asked him to take the assignment. Their magazine was doing a special feature on cats, with one section on cats and travel. Taketomi-jima was one of the possible sites, but the company didn't have the budget to send their own in-house photographer on the assignment. So they picked one they knew who'd moved to Okinawa.

Taketomijima would later become better known as an island with a lot of cats, but back then it had not yet become famous, and the editorial staff had done a good job in spotting its potential before anyone else.

"That sounds good, Katsu-san. You like animals, don't you?"

Haruko still had a lot to learn about my father, I thought.

"I guess, but . . . if it's for work . . . Cats and I don't exactly hit it off . . ."

"Oh, so you don't like cats?"

My father seemed at a loss for a reply, so I piped up. "Dad doesn't dislike cats, but they don't usually like *him*."

"Shut up!" Dad growled as he gulped down some of the Okinawan *chanpuru* stir-fry he'd piled on top of his rice.

His problem with cats was that he overdid it with the touching and playing. He'd rush over to them and they'd run away. Or else hiss in anger.

"Dogs I'm better with," he added.

Still, even with dogs, the ones that would respond well to him were the gentler types, or older. Dogs that were bashful around strangers felt scared by him, and hard-to-please dogs would bark.

In the past we'd visited Nara, famous for its deer, and when he rushed at one, crying out, *It's Bambi!* an angry parent deer had bulldozed him aside.

I was wondering whether to tell Haruko about this incident—but when I remembered that my late mother had been with us at the time, I decided not to.

"If they were salamanders, you might be able to photograph them well," I teased.

But Dad took it seriously. "Yeah, they don't seem to run away so fast." As a photographer, maybe you shouldn't admit defeat like that.

"If all of us go, it should be at the weekend or on holiday." Haruko laid down her chopsticks and started leafing through her planner. For most school holidays, she had to work as a guide.

"The weekend after next I have free. That Monday is Founders' Day, so we could stay for two nights and three days. Does that sound good?"

She was referring to Founders' Day for my elementary school. It wasn't on the calendar, so until Haruko mentioned it, I'd totally forgotten about it.

So Haruko had all my school activities written down in her planner, did she? The thought made me a bit uneasy. She had all these written down in her planner because she'd become my *mother*. She cooked for me every day, washed my clothes. And whenever there was a school event, there she was. If it was up to Dad, he'd get all the notifications and info messed up, that was obvious, so it was the correct division of labor.

Every day, Haruko was being my *mother*.

So how long would I keep calling her *Haruko-san?*

I still felt confused about calling her *Mom*. It was only two years since my mother had passed away.

Haruko didn't say anything, and always smiled cheerfully, and I let her spoil me, and got away without calling her *Mom*.

"Okay, then, the week after next," Dad said, excited at the prospect. Our trip to Cat Island was set.

 ༄

It was sunny, fortunately, on the day we departed.

We took the first flight of the day from Naha to Ishigaki-jima, then a thirty-minute bus ride from Ishigakijima airport to where we would catch the ferry. Haruko had arranged for all the transfers to be smooth, so barely three hours after we'd left home, we were on the high-speed boat to Cat Island.

As ever, the color of the sea around Okinawa shimmered turquoise. The thing that surprised me most after we moved wasn't all the incredible tropical flowers, or the blazing light, but the harbors.

Even the sea filling each little harbor was a bright blue, as if paint had been dissolved into it. This blue, like colored water a child would make for fun, spread all the way from the wharf to the far-off shore.

The high-speed boat seemed to fly over this unbelievable turquoise sea like a stone skipping across the water. It took about ten minutes to reach the island.

Thinking he needed to be taking photos of the scenery, Dad had been snapping away since before we got on the ferry.

The boat arrived at the pier at Taketomijima and we and our fellow passengers all crowded off. Here small shuttle buses were waiting to pick up guests already booked into the local inns. It was a tiny island, a mere 9.2 kilometers in circumference, and so there were no taxis.

While passengers were getting into their various rides, we waited for Dad to take his photos.

"Where are all the cats?" I asked Haruko as we waited in the shade for him to finish. I'd been picturing cats lined up at the harbor to greet us, and felt a bit disappointed.

"There are plenty of them in the villages and around the beach. People don't linger at the harbor, so that's why."

Even if they decided to take up residence here, they wouldn't reap much from the tourists in the way of food.

A van had just pulled up at the bus stop and Haruko waved at it.

"I asked them to come when you were about to finish taking pictures, Katsu-san," she said.

She'd timed it perfectly. Before they got married, Haruko had been Dad's guide many times on photo trips to Okinawa.

The van trundled along slowly, but it was still only a matter of minutes before we had arrived at the village in the center of the island. We hadn't yet passed a single car.

The asphalt road began to peter out and now we were driving along a road of white sand that weaved its way past a terrace of houses with their low stone walls and the distinctive Okinawan red tiles, *shisa* guardian lion figures perching on the roofs.

The van pulled in front of a house with particularly crazy-looking *shisa* on its roof.

"Oh, I'm so happy you chose this one," my father said excitedly. "The first time Haruko ever guided me on a photo trip, this was the place we stayed," he added.

"It looks like an ordinary house . . . Is it like a guesthouse?" I asked. For a guesthouse it seemed quite cozy, as if one family would barely fit inside.

Haruko explained. "People have family homes in Taketomijima that they rent out to tourists. Think of it as a kind of holiday cottage."

Apparently an acquaintance of Haruko's managed it as a part-time business.

My father leaped out of the van in high spirits and started heaving our luggage out with the help of the driver. What with all the camera equipment we had more bags than your usual family on a three-day trip.

Haruko strode across the lawn and thrust her hand into a gap in the stone wall. After a rummage, she brought out a wooden tag with a key attached. The whole setup was so analog, I exclaimed in surprise and Haruko smiled.

"When they're here they hand me the key, but when they're not, this is how we do it."

"And that's okay? No one minds on the island?" I meant in terms of security.

"No one minds," she confirmed.

"I guess it's unlikely there are any thieves who'd bother coming all this way."

Once we had stepped into the house, you could take in the whole of the interior in a single glance. Three tatami rooms, a tiny kitchen, and beyond that what I imagined must be the bathroom. Just right for one family.

So they had stayed here together before, I mused. Dad had come on a photo trip to Okinawa for the first time about six months after Mom died.

Just as I was thinking this, Haruko smiled and whispered, "I stayed at a different friend's house."

"Oh!" I nodded and went over to the front door to help Dad haul in the luggage. Our van had already left.

"Were you able to get some good cat shots the last time you were here?" I asked him.

"Cats weren't what I was after then."

The assignment had apparently been to photograph typical island scenery to go in a guidebook, with cats just as an added extra.

They had laid out three sets of futons for us, which had been aired in a dryer and were nice and fluffy.

"Oh—this'll be the first time we'll all sleep lined up in one room together."

It's when he says things like that that Dad makes me feel bad. I wasn't sure if, out of duty to my mom, I should have whined a bit about the sleeping arrangements. He should have just let it pass without comment.

"This room faces east and the rising sun feels really good. We can look forward to getting up in the morning," said Haruko. Now I no longer needed to make a fuss about the sleeping arrangements. I was looking forward to getting up in the morning, too.

"We have all the ingredients, so I'll whip together something for lunch."

The fridge and kitchen shelves were packed. The system was that the owner stocked whatever food they thought appropriate, and we could help ourselves. All the necessities were provided, making you feel really at home, like staying at a relative's house where they had laid on everything.

"Well, I'm going to go rent us some bicycles," Dad said.

Tourists on the island mainly got around either on foot or using rental bikes. You could call the bike shop and they'd bring them over, but since the shop was nearby, Dad said he'd go for a walk and drop in on the way.

"Why don't you leave the camera behind?" Haruko said. "I'm making *somen chanpuru* and it will be ready soon."

"Don't worry. I won't be long," Dad said and set off, a camera slung over his shoulder.

"I'd better reckon on about thirty minutes, I guess."

Haruko's prediction was on the right track. If he came back in thirty minutes, that would be fast for him.

"Ryo-chan, you should go check out the area, too," she said to me.

"I might sleep for a while," I replied.

We'd got up so early, I was feeling a bit sleepy. And the beach chair for lounging in the garden looked pretty inviting.

I went out into the garden and lay down but then quickly got up again as the sun was shining right in my eyes. I tried moving the chair around and adjusting the angle of the back, searching for a comfortable position.

I'd finally found the best spot when I saw someone gazing at me from the gate. It was a bent-over old woman. She must live in the neighborhood, I reckoned, but she was scrutinizing me so intently I began to feel uncomfortable.

"Excuse me, but may I help you?" I got up and walked over to the old woman. With a jolt, I saw that her right eye was all cloudy.

The old woman seemed to notice how I tried to hide my shock and brought up a hand to cover her right eye. "I'm sorry if it makes you feel bad."

"No, I'm okay." I may have said this, but it's true I was taken aback.

"I was sick when I was a child," she explained.

She apparently couldn't see at all out of her right eye, and I thought how hard it must have been for her to live with this all her life.

"Are the people you came with your parents?"

She seemed to be referring to Dad and Haruko. Did she know them? I wondered.

"I'm my father's child from a previous marriage."

"Ah, I see. That explains it. Even if they had a child soon after they got married, you're a bit too big."

So she *did* know them. "Are you friendly with my dad and Haruko?" I asked.

"You might say that," the old woman answered vaguely. "Are you all happy?" she added.

This sudden question threw me completely, and I fumbled for an answer. Did she mean me? Or Dad? Or Haruko?

"Haruko is cooking right now. And Dad went out to hire rental bikes for us . . ."

My reply was as weird as if I'd said *Once upon a time there was a grandpa and grandma, and the grandpa went out gathering firewood in the hills while Granny stayed by the river washing clothes*, like some old folktale. I mentioned Haruko first since she was in the house. I thought maybe the woman wanted me to fetch her.

The old woman's face creased into a smile, buried so deep in all the wrinkles it took me a moment to realize.

"I'm glad you're all happy." I hadn't said anything about us being happy. "I was a bit concerned about them, you see."

"If you want to have a chat with Haruko, she's here. Should I get her?"

"Nah, that's fine," she said, brushing off the question, and abruptly walked away. I stood there, watching her shuffle off.

I made my way back to the beach chair I'd spent so long getting in the right position and flopped down on it.

A few minutes later Dad came back.

"Hey, Ryo. You look very cozy."

"Dad! If you'd got here a few moments ago, you'd have seen someone you know."

"Oh, really? Who?"

"An old lady."

I hesitated to mention her cloudy eye. "Her sight wasn't so good," is how I put it, but Dad didn't seem to have a clue.

"Someone Haruko knows, maybe." He stepped into the house with a quizzical look on his face. I followed after him.

"Ohh—good timing." Haruko's voice greeted us from the kitchen. "It's just about ready."

The smell of *somen chanpuru* being sautéed in sesame oil wafted toward us.

"Someone you know stopped by, apparently. An old lady."

"I wonder who it was. Saying it's an old lady doesn't really tell me anything . . ."

"She had a bad eye," I added, but that didn't seem to help narrow down the field.

"That's not uncommon."

"Well, I guess she might come by again since she lives in the neighborhood."

"Yes, maybe," Haruko said, carrying two plates of noodles. She placed them in front of us, and I fetched the third plate and set it down for Haruko.

"You have one hand free, so you could have brought the chopsticks." Dad got up after me and came back in with three sets of disposable chopsticks.

"You have a hand free, so you could have brought the tea, too." Haruko smiled and headed back to the kitchen. She came back balancing two cups neatly in one hand as I went to fetch the third cup from the kitchen.

"Don't they have a tray?" Dad asked. Maybe he was feeling a bit ashamed, having brought back only the chopsticks.

"No, there isn't one. Even though they've provided pretty much everything else. I'll let the owner know, since it'll be nice for others who stay here."

Even though she had cooked it in someone else's kitchen, the *somen chanpuru*, made with canned tuna, onions and carrots, tasted just as if she had cooked it at home.

The food was delicious, but Dad still had to say, "You know, when we make *chanpuru*, I'd like to include some of those island spring onions, too."

Haruko had recently rustled up a special dish of sautéed spring onions and bacon mixed with noodles. Spring onions went well with any kind of noodle—*somen chanpuru*, spaghetti, yakisoba, whatever.

"If you go shopping over at Ishigakijima, buy some and I'll make it," Haruko said, letting any perceived negative comment pass. There wasn't a supermarket on Taketomijima, and the islanders went over to Ishigakijima by boat to do their shopping.

"The tuna works well, too, so just be quiet and eat," I said.

Dad and I often had this kind of reversal of roles, where I said what an adult would say as if he were the child. My late mother used to tell him, laughingly, "Take a lesson from Ryo."

Haruko and my mother shared this trait, being able to accept my often childlike father. In other words, the capacity for patience and generosity needed to be Dad's wife.

Haruko let it all go as a joke, but my mom, an elementary school teacher, would smilingly tell him to not be so selfish. When I thought about this, I realized it was one of the reasons why I found it hard to call Haruko *Mom*.

Mom and Haruko were similar, I realized. They might express themselves differently, but what lay behind their words was very similar. A warmth, a gentleness, a generosity, a bigheartedness . . . that was the very least of it.

If they had had more contrasting personalities, aside from whether I could actually open up or not, I might have been able to come to a decision more quickly. But the uncanny resemblance between them made Haruko overlap with Mom in my mind. In a sense, Dad's taste in women remained steady, you could say.

And it was because Haruko and Mom were so similar that, every time I was on the verge of calling Haruko *Mom*, confusion and hesitation took hold of me.

While we were having our meal, a small truck pulled up outside with our rental bikes. Three red city bicycles, the kind with baskets on the front.

Haruko seemed to know the deliveryman and went out to sign the receipt.

. .

Immediately after we'd finished eating, we set out in search of cats.

"Maybe we should bring some food for them?" I said as we stepped out of the house, the thought just occurring to me.

"Great idea!" Dad said. I don't think he was all that confident the cats would take to him.

Naturally there was no designated cat food in the house, so we rummaged around for something the cats would like.

We picked out some *chikuwa* fish cakes and processed cheese, which Haruko cut up into small pieces and placed in a plastic ziplock bag. We then set off on our rental bikes.

"The tires can get stuck in the sand, so be careful not to fall," Dad instructed me, though with his camera bag slung over his shoulder and single-lens reflex camera hanging from his neck, *he* looked like the one who was about to topple over.

The sand along the alleyways lay quite thick, and we couldn't glide down as on a paved road. On both sides, our tires would sink into the sand, making ruts and slowing us down. We were heading to a particular beach that was said to have a lot of cats. It was about five minutes by bike from our house. Once we'd got out of the village, we emerged onto a paved road that encircled the island. Over time this road, too, had begun to crack and weeds were shooting up.

We carried on pedaling, over a stretch of compacted sand. Just beyond, we caught sight of the sparkling blue water. We parked our bikes, close to the water's edge, near a mini arbor.

As we walked closer, we saw them. Over twenty, at least. Kittens and grown-up cats. Everywhere. As many as thirty of them.

"I see them, I see them!"

Dad rushed toward the arbor. The cats, cooling off in the shade, began to creep stealthily backward at the sight of this excited old guy intruding on their space.

"Damn, they don't like me."

Haruko and I walked tentatively toward them; the cats didn't move a whisker.

A black-and-white tuxedo cat lay flat on a nearby bench, its paws folded under. Haruko stroked it lightly with her fingertips; the cat waved its tail once in response.

"Oh, that's what I would like to do. Just casually pet them," Dad said.

"Then just go ahead," Haruko said, laughing.

Dad reached out, but the tuxedo cat furrowed its brow, turned its head away and leaped off the bench.

"See. I don't know why, but they always do that to me." It was hardly surprising—he was too forceful about trying to pet them. "Ah, but today I have a secret weapon." Dad took out the plastic bag filled with food from his camera bag.

I was the one who'd suggested bringing food along, Haruko was the one who'd prepared the food, but Dad was the one who made use of it. He was quite shameless about taking a piece of the action. He wasn't even aware of it. I guess that's what you had to expect from a child.

"Are you going to feed them now?" Haruko asked.

"When else am I supposed to?" Dad laughed. "Hey, guys, here's some food for you. It's really tasty!"

Dad opened up the bag and the ears of the cats shot straight up and swiveled toward the source of the sound. From every direction all eyes were focused on him. The cats waiting at a distance began to pad forward. Dad was swiftly and silently encircled.

Instinctively, I backed off a bit, moving over toward Haruko. These prowling cats weren't about to cutely coax any food from him. The scene reminded me of something. A TV documentary about wild animals that hunt in packs and behave just like this . . .

"Ha ha ha, they're just cats, after all. Isn't it cute how they're going for the food!"

Innocent, triumphant, Dad pulled some tidbits from the plastic bag. Just at that moment—the pack moved. Swarming around Dad from all directions. Not a single sweetly begging *meow*, but the whole pack advancing with silent intent, an awful energy focused on Dad, demanding that he *hand it over*.

"What the—?"

Dad began to shake and dropped a piece of *chikuwa* fish cake. It rolled away on the ground. A number of cats made a dash for it and it quickly disappeared into one of their mouths.

The cats closed in further on Dad, moving to cut him off. One bold cat reached up and batted at Dad's knuckles. Another made a leap for the plastic bag. All a bit demonic.

"Haruko-san! These guys are harassing me!"

"They're wild animals."

"Get back!" Dad tossed some bits of food further out. The siege fell apart as a number of cats dashed toward the tidbits rolling on the ground. Others were anticipating that Dad was still holding more food. They gathered in an even tighter circle around him. Exactly as if they were on the hunt.

"Whoa—!"

In a flash, a particularly brazen cat had yanked the plastic bag from Dad's hands. The food scattered and the cats ran amok. A massive brown tiger cat, clearly the boss, growled at his companions as he gulped down his food.

"Hey, you! You've had plenty! Give some to the kittens!" Dad shouted, and when he tried to shoo the boss away, the cat flashed its front claws. It raked Dad's right hand and left other notable scratches.

In an instant, the cats had devoured the food, and their wild frenzy began to subside. They scattered to their preferred spots and collapsed.

"You damn cats!" Dad railed at them. They'd grabbed all his food for free and he hadn't managed to get a single photo.

"But I thought you said they were cute," Haruko teased.

"Those are—wild animals."

"It's not easy for them to survive, you know. The islanders feed them, but it's never enough, and the stronger ones get most of it."

"So that boss cat's always eating. He should share some with the smaller cats."

"That logic doesn't work in the wild." I couldn't help a jab at Dad.

"I mean, you should have warned me that they were going to be so fierce." Dad directed his petulance at Haruko.

"Well, I didn't think you were going to feed them right there and then," Haruko said. "I was sure you'd take the bag out to feed a smaller group or if you saw a kitten by itself."

It's true Haruko had expressed her surprise that he was feeding them so quickly. She'd known there was going to be carnage.

"Enough of this." Dad was beginning to sulk. "I can take photos without the need to bribe them. I'm a professional. Plus I have a telephoto lens."

As he was speaking, Dad started to change lenses. He did this not in the cats' headquarters, the arbor, but safely outside on a bench.

When he finally started on his photo shoot, both Dad and the cats were professional about it, Dad nifty behind the camera, the cats natural at lounging and licking, staring into the distance and lazily twitching their tails.

When Dad suppressed his desire to touch the cats and just focused on photographing them, they went about their business, oblivious to him, grooming, napping and enjoying their space.

Nowadays with digital cameras you can take as many photos as you like and curate them later, but at the time analog cameras were what most people used, and you wouldn't know how well the photos you had taken would turn out until they were developed. Each photo cost money, so it wasn't so easy to continuously click the shutter. Photographers showed their stuff when they captured the perfect moment.

Dozing, contented cats, the occasional click of the shutter when Dad, in his own way, thought the moment was right.

"I'd like to see a little more movement," he muttered after a while. Left to their own devices, the cats sprawled listlessly, showing no intention of doing anything interesting for the camera.

With his telephoto lens he did follow a couple of kittens who were climbing on each other's backs as they headed playfully toward the beach, but back at the arbor things remained laid-back.

"Ryo, could you engage with one of them for a bit? As if you're an island kid playing with a cat?"

"No way!" I replied in an instant. "It'll be in a magazine, right?"

A more outgoing child would have leaped at the chance, but I wasn't one of them, and there was no way I wanted to be featured in a magazine. No, thanks.

"The editor will make the final selection, so there's no guarantee."

"But it might. So I don't want to. I mean, it would be fake, anyway. I'm not an islander or anything."

"Then how about we list you as a child of one of the tourists?"

"*No. Way!*"

Dad and I kept sparring until we heard a loud flutter of flapping wings coming from the beach.

"*Noooo!*" It was Haruko screaming.

The kittens on the beach were now surrounded by crows. One kitten had failed to get away and they were pecking at it.

"Get away, you—!" Dad put his camera down and scurried toward the beach. In times like this, he could really move. Haruko took off after him.

The two adults had vanished, leaving the expensive camera equipment behind them, so I ended up staying behind to mind it. We couldn't just leave Dad's camera, no matter how laid-back the island was.

"*Gya—!*" Dad yelled as the crows tried to attack him.

"Hang on, Katsu-san!" Haruko, arms windmilling, joined in as the crows continued their assault.

"They never change, those two." I turned at the sound of the voice behind me and saw the old woman I'd met earlier. The brightness of the sea and sand made her cloudy, whitish eye stand out even more.

"Never change?"

"When they came the last time, they did the same thing, getting all flustered trying to save something that didn't need to be saved."

"That didn't need to be saved . . ."

Wasn't it just human nature to try to save a poor little cat being pecked at by crows?

"The weak get hunted down. That's the way it is." The old woman's words were heartless but for some reason didn't feel harsh.

"If the weak don't die, things will come to a dead end."

What would come to a dead end? I didn't dare ask. It felt like if I did, I'd get some terrible, bleak response.

"So have they tried to rescue a kitten before?"

"It was a fully grown cat. It had lived a long life, and it would have been okay if it had gone."

"Damn it!" My dad's cries came from the beach. He was throwing sand at the crows.

"Ryo, get some stones!"

"What?"

I looked around. The ground around the arbor was sandy; there were no stones big enough to use.

"I can see some over there." The old woman pointed at a thicket with a line of low shrubs.

I hesitated. I wanted to hear more of what she had to say. What would this old woman, with her heartless vision, make of Dad and Haruko? I was especially curious about when Dad and Haruko first met. And about how they had rescued a grown cat that had lived long enough.

"Go on," the old woman urged me. "If you want to hear more, go out into the garden and look at the stars this evening. I take walks around there at night, too."

It turned out that while I was gathering stones for a counterattack, our intervention had already made the crows give up on the kitten.

"Not a word of thanks from him, even though we saved his life," muttered Dad.

As soon as the crows had flown off, the kitten made a desperate dash back toward the arbor.

"What do you expect? It's a cat living out in nature," Haruko said, laughing, and without thinking I came back with, "Since it's part of nature, isn't it better not to rescue it?"

The old woman's words had stayed with me.

The weak get hunted down. That's the way it is . . . If the weak don't die, things will come to a dead end.

"I suppose so," Haruko said with a smile. "But us being here is also a natural part of things."

"You're right!" Dad said, interrupting. "That kitten was lucky. If your luck's good, you get saved; if not, you die. That's fine. I mean, you would have a guilty conscience if you just stood by and watched crows peck a defenseless kitten to death, right? Especially during what's meant to be a relaxing family trip."

"Isn't this trip a work-related photo shoot?" I said.

"It's a family trip which I'm paying for, so that's entirely within the scope of my discretion!"

The lucky little kitten had by now been absorbed by the group and we could no longer see which one it was. There might be days when the crows came out on top and the kitten didn't. Today, however, it was lucky—the logic was simple and I completely understood.

Dad and Haruko lived according to the same logic. That's the thought that occurred to me.

Dad lingered at the beach until evening.

A few tourists wandered by, some of whom fell prey to the cats just as Dad had, and occasionally mini spats broke out among the cats.

Camera in hand, he caught it all.

"That's one clumsy cat." Dad pointed to a beautiful brown tabby with well-defined markings around the eyes. He wasn't as tiny as a kitten, nor as large as the fully grown cats. Must be around six months old, was Haruko's guess.

Haruko and I noticed something about that brown tabby. Perhaps because his position in the group was tenuous, when tourists dropped by with food the other cats would growl at him and drive him away, even before they went for the food.

Whenever a tidbit happened to land nearby, he'd hesitate and, in that instant, it would be snatched away.

"I wish we still had some food."

Dad had spotted how some tourists offered food to the cats they liked most. They'd scatter tidbits to distract the main group of cats, and approach the single cat they had picked out. Then they'd bring food hidden in their hand, crouch down casually and drop it by their paws.

"Using that method you should be able to target that clumsy cat and get him some food," he suggested.

The sun had turned a luminous orange. Dad changed the exposure setting on his camera and squinted, hoping to catch the cats and the setting sun together.

Right then I made a great discovery.

"Dad," I called quietly, but he'd noticed, too.

A cat had backed into the low line of shrubs. In its jaws was a plover, the bird's head hanging down limply.

The cat had withdrawn into the bushes so the others wouldn't attempt to grab it. And wonder of wonders, this cat was the clumsy brown tabby.

Dad continued clicking the shutter.

The brown tabby had now safely brought its catch into the bushes. An unlucky plover. With the brown tabby it wasn't luck, but skill. It was the plover's bad luck to have caught the eye of a hunter.

"What do you expect? He's wild," Dad murmured.

Being lucky. Being unlucky. Being skilled. Each of these combined to determine who survived in this tiny wild kingdom that coexisted beside the humans.

"Should we go back?"

Dad put down his camera. He'd taken the best photo of the day.

On the way home, a few cats were padding around, but Dad left his camera in its case.

．．

For dinner Haruko used whatever was in the fridge to rustle up tofu *chanpuru* and papaya *irichi*.

"Ryo-chan, do you want to have a bath first?" she asked as she tidied up after the meal.

"I'll have it later. Is it okay if I lie out in the garden?"

"It can get pretty chilly here at night."

"I thought if I lie down on the beach chair, I'll get a good view of the stars."

"That sounds good," Haruko said, allowing me to enjoy the cool of the evening as long as I wrapped myself in a blanket.

"That looks nice. I might check the stars out myself," my dad said, seeing me cozily ensconced in my chair.

There were two beach chairs lined up in the garden, but I said, "You should have a bath first. If we both put it off, then Haruko won't be able to have one until much later."

Haruko always had a bath last. She liked to drain the water when she was done and do a quick scrub of the tub.

"But if I have a bath first and then join you outside, I might catch a cold. I want to see the stars, too, you know."

What a child he is.

"If you dry your hair well and wrap yourself in a towel, you should be okay."

"I'll get another bottle of beer ready for you when you get out of the bath," Haruko said, joining forces with me, and somehow we managed to hustle Dad back inside the house.

· ·

I had no idea when the old woman would pass by on her walk, but old people tend to go to bed pretty early, so I figured it wouldn't be that late. We'd finished dinner, and it was a little before eight p.m. If the old woman did go for a walk, this would be about the right time. So if I didn't see her, it would mean I was just unlucky.

When I lay down on the beach chair, the stars looked surprisingly close, as if they would fall to the ground at any moment.

If I turned off the porch light, I could see them even better, I realized, so I went back inside for a second and hit the switch. And *wow!*—the stars now looked close enough to touch. I lay sprawled on the beach chair, for all the world like a king.

I began to recall snatches of the Tanabata song of the Star Festival, when the celestial lovers would meet once a year. It described the stars as gold and silver powder sprinkled across the sky.

"Ah, so you're there, are you." Over by the gate, the old woman peeked in.

"You said you take walks at night, and so I thought it'd be around now."

"Good thinking," she said.

"Here, you can sit down." I motioned for her to come through the gate, which she did and sat down on the other beach chair.

"We were talking about those two, weren't we?"

And the old woman launched into the story of when Dad
and Haruko first came to the island.

᠄ᢧ

Dad had arrived on the island looking totally dispirited, she
said.

From the moment they met, Haruko had been worried
about him. This was the first time he'd visited Okinawa, and it
was, unfortunately, rainy from the start. Quite stormy, in fact.
Haruko suggested that he take advantage of the weather to
photograph Okinawa in a storm, and took him to a spot well
known for its large waves.

I'd heard all this before and figured it must have been a
good trip.

But the old woman shook her head. "Far from it," she said.
"Your father looked in bad shape. As if his *mapui*, his soul, had
fallen away."

The idea that the soul could fall away was a concept unique
to Okinawa, where they believed it could be triggered by a
great shock or surprise. In that event, you had to pick up the
fallen soul and return it to the body. If you didn't, you'd become depressed, your body would start to ache and, in the
worst case, you could become seriously ill.

I knew the reason why Dad's soul had fallen away. Mom
had died, and he was at a total loss. To escape from the reality

of her death, he'd traveled all over Japan taking photographs, like a kind of pilgrimage.

When he first met Haruko, his soul had probably still not returned to his body.

"Your mom took such loving care of him, you know."

I was still uncomfortable hearing Haruko referred to as my *mom*, but I didn't tell the old woman this. Legally, Haruko was already my mother, and a child complaining to a third party soon after his father remarried was itself pretty childish.

I wouldn't be able to laugh at Dad anymore for being such a *child*.

The old woman went on. The storm began to clear, but soon enough, the seas around the island began to turn rough and choppy as a new storm approached. Dad gave up photographing the sea, which had begun to look murky, and spent his time taking pictures of the houses with their red roof tiles.

On that visit, Dad had stayed in this very same house. Haruko seemed to regret that she hadn't booked him into a regular inn that provided meals.

"I'll come back later so we can wander around the island at night, so have some dinner first. You can eat any of the food stocked in the house. If it's too much trouble to cook, there's always cup ramen."

After several reminders, Haruko left, seemingly still a bit concerned.

"She asked me to keep an eye on him when she left," the old

woman said with a laugh. "She must have been quite worried to ask the neighbors to look out for him."

Haruko ended up coming back earlier than she'd planned. She'd packed a few dishes in Tupperware containers for him to eat.

The lights were still on.

"Mr. Sakamoto," she called at the front door, but Dad wasn't in. Pushing open the door and entering, she came across a note lying on the low table in the living room.

I've gone to watch the ocean.

A guidebook was left open on the table at the page that described the pier on the west side.

Haruko placed the Tupperware boxes in the fridge and sat down to wait, but there was no sign of his return. She decided to go to the western pier to find him.

"It turned out I went along with her," the old woman said, somewhat cryptically.

The western pier lay in darkness. He said he was going to watch the ocean, but that was impossible. The sea was completely black, and everything offshore was lost in darkness. Great waves broke against the pier, the spray glittering white in the moonlight.

Dad was seated at the base of the pier, looking vacant. Relieved, Haruko walked over to him.

"Mr. Sakamoto," she called, and he looked up. Haruko stopped walking. Dad's face was wet with tears.

"Uh, the thing is . . ." he said, hurriedly wiping his face. "I happened to be remembering my late wife. Pretty unseemly, huh," he added, sniffing. "I know it's time to get over it, but still . . ."

All Haruko could do was stand silently beside him.

"My son's much stronger than I am. I'm just a no-good . . ."

"It must have been so hard for you," Haruko murmured, the words just slipping out.

And then, shoulders heaving, Dad began to sob uncontrollably.

Haruko crouched down beside him, stroking his back. It was an entirely natural gesture, as if she were treating someone who had been wounded. If there's someone injured in front of you, it's human nature to go to them.

Dad continued to wail.

Haruko remained beside him until the tears finally began to slow.

"I'll head back to your lodgings," she said. "So please take your time." And she left.

Dad gave himself up to the tears that overwhelmed him once again.

Time passed, but still no sign of Dad.

Haruko waited almost an hour before going back out to the pier to get him. She was worried, the way he'd been sobbing so relentlessly.

When she reached him, she found him standing, stock-still, on the beach.

She watched as he started to run toward the sea. Haruko tried to call out, but her voice cracked. She raced after him.

Dad pushed through the waves straight into the sea.

"Mr. Sakamoto!"

Dad kept wading.

Splashing feverishly through the waves, Haruko finally made it to his side. The sea was still shallow at this point, the water up to her chest.

"Come back!" she cried, but the wind snatched her words away. The waves beating against her, she grabbed Dad by the collar.

"Think about your son, before you go after her!"

"L-let go of me . . ."

"No!"

"The cat!" he yelled. "It's going to die!"

She looked over to where he was pointing, where the waves were crashing against the pier, the spray surging upward.

A cat was floundering in the waves.

Half wading, half swimming, Dad and Haruko together managed to scoop up the drowning cat. The waves tossed them about as they made their way back to shore.

"This doesn't look good," Dad said. The drenched cat lay limp in his arms, its eyes closed.

"It must have swallowed a lot of water."

"How do you do CPR on a cat?" Dad asked, and then dangled the cat by its rear legs, giving it a vigorous shake up and down.

"That's not the way to do it," said Haruko. "When kids choke on a sweet, this is what you do. You slap them firmly a few times between the shoulder blades. Do it right and they'll spit it out."

Dad's emergency treatment actually worked and the cat began to vomit up water. Having got all the water out, it collapsed in exhaustion.

"We should take it back to our place."

"Good idea. It's cold here."

Dad and Haruko both looked like soaked rats themselves.

Back at the house, they showered the cat with warm water and dried it off with towels and a hair dryer.

They made a bed for the cat in a cardboard box and put it down to sleep, then the two of them took turns having a shower. Dad rummaged around in the closet and came up with a pair of pajamas, which Haruko put on.

Once they'd both changed, the cat, too, had settled—no longer a half-drowned wreck but simply an ordinary sleeping cat, sacked out for the night.

Um . . ." Haruko began awkwardly later. "I'm sorry. I totally misunderstood what was going on."

"Don't worry at all, it's okay," Dad said, himself apologetic. "Of course you'd think that—with a grown-up man bawling his eyes out, and then walking out to sea."

He peered into the cardboard box.

"This cat seems to have eye problems."

"I think you're right. And it must live somewhere nearby."

"It sort of hung around me for a while when I was down at the pier, and after I'd stopped crying, it started wandering around. Then it lost its footing and fell off the pier."

"It's because it followed me. I shouldn't have let it," said Haruko.

"No, it's my fault. It really seemed to want to hang around me."

"No, I'm to blame."

"No—it's my fault."

They argued for a while, then finally looked at each other and burst out laughing.

"What should we do about the night excursion we were planning around the island?" Haruko asked.

"Let's save that for next time," Dad said. "Please take me around then. I'll bring my son with me."

"I'd love to. I look forward to it." Still worried about his dinner, Haruko added on her way out, "I put some food in the fridge for you."

∽

What a dumb, clumsy cat. Imagine losing its footing and falling into the sea—its time was up, I'd say." No words of sympathy for the cat from the old woman.

"It was lucky." I went with Dad and Haruko's logic. "It was natural, too, that Dad and Haruko got together."

A wild kingdom right next to where people lived. If humans dropped in every once in a while, well, that was okay.

"Luck . . . right. Well, I guess we'll just leave it at that." The old woman chuckled. "After all that commotion, it seems your father's *mapui* came back. That makes sense. Right," she added. "If you do something for other people, it'll be good for you, too."

It wasn't *people*, though, in this case, but a cat.

With a grunt, the old woman got to her feet.

"Shall I go and fetch Dad and Haruko?" I asked.

"No, it's fine. I'd better get back or the people at home will start to worry."

The old woman shuffled slowly over to the gate. After a moment, she turned around.

"Are you going to start calling her *Mom* soon?"

"What?"

"Someone's waiting for it."

I knew, of course. That Dad was wanting me to call Haruko *Mom*.

"Very patient, they are, so I don't think they'll be pushing you into it."

"What?" I blurted out again.

Patient? Since when does that describe Dad?

"By *they*, do you mean Haruko?"

There was no reply, for the old woman had tottered out of the gate.

. .

I was standing there, stock-still, when Haruko came outside.
"Ryo-chan, time for your bath."

"My turn, my turn," Dad said as he came outside. His hair
was dried, and he was holding a bottle of beer. "Whoa, now
this is a bed fit for a king," he murmured as he sank into the
beach chair, his reaction the same as mine.

The next day we made another trip around the island in
search of cats.

There were cats living on a beach where you could scoop up
star-shaped grains of sand; Dad photographed the cats from
many different angles. We competed to see who could scoop
up the most star-shaped sand, and predictably Dad was the one
who took it far too seriously.

That evening we went on our final excursion to the arbor.
The beach lay glowing white in the moonlight, while the cats
lay stretched out at random.

"This is a scene you don't see every day," Dad said, quickly
setting up his tripod, and snapping the cats on a slow shutter
speed.

On a slower setting of twenty seconds, the lens took in that
much more light, making the night look even more astonish-
ing, with the available light coming only from the moon and
stars.

Even after he had stowed away the camera, we sat motion-
less on the beach, gazing at the cats.

"Finally, we managed to get around the entire island at night," Dad commented.

We'll go around the island at night at the next opportunity. Someday, I'll bring my son.

His last trip to Cat Island had ended with this promise.

"Back then . . . you rescued a cat from a stormy sea, didn't you?" I started to speak but then swallowed my words.

The story about how Dad had cried his eyes out over my dead mother. Not the right story to bring up when we were on a family trip like this with Haruko.

"What?" Dad asked, urging me to go on, and I changed tack.

"So before, when you were here, you didn't walk around the island at night?"

This was all I could do to change tack and not make it sound weird. I mean, I was a kid, after all.

Dad and Haruko exchanged a look, and then the faintest of smiles.

"When I was here before . . . there was a big storm and the waves were huge," said Dad.

Which was true, but not the whole story. Not by a long shot.

This is how adults smooth out certain topics, I realized. So even Dad had some adult qualities after all, I thought.

"I wanted you to be there the next time I visited, Ryo."

Yeah, I know, I thought, but left the rest unsaid.

"I'm glad we could all be here together."

Not the whole story. But it wasn't a lie.

. .

Dad had taken enough photographs of cats, so the next day we decided to wander around Ishigakijima before heading home.

We left our lodgings in time to make the ferry arriving at the island just after nine a.m.

Haruko left the key in the same spot as before, and we were loading our luggage into the van that had come for us when an elderly cat came tottering up the sandy path toward us.

It was a black tabby, its paler patches of fur yellowed by the sun and the sea.

"Goodness!" Haruko shouted. "Katsu-san, look!"

Dad took a good look at the cat. "Well, what do you know," he said. "So how've you been?"

The old cat meekly let Dad pet it, super friendly as it rubbed its cheeks and the top of its head against his hand.

"When we were here last time, this cat was about to drown, and Katsu-san rescued it."

Yeah, I know, I thought, without saying so. "I've seen it several times."

The cat's right eye was whitish, and clouded over.

"So you're still living around here, eh?" said Dad.

"A little while after that, one of the neighbors took it in," said Haruko.

"Really? Lucky you, eh? You'll spend your final days nice and snug."

As if to say *thanks to you*, the cat rubbed its head even more vigorously against Dad's hand. It began to push its flank against Haruko, too, and me as well.

"Thank you," I murmured. "Thank you for telling me so many stories. I'll call her *Mom* soon," I whispered as I dug my fingers into its side, and the cat rubbed its whole body against me, right side and left, backward and forward, as if it was praising me for my decision.

∽

The day after we got back home, Dad wasted no time in printing out the photographs and sending them to his magazine editor.

A month later, we received copies of the special cat issue.

As Dad flipped through its pages, he began to frown, then he looked up at the ceiling. "Ah—damn it!"

Haruko and I both peered over at the magazine and knew in an instant what he meant. The single photo Dad was most proud of had been left out—the one of the hunter with the plover in its mouth.

The photos they had used were of the cats playing on the beach at night, and pictures of cute little kittens. He was paid the same no matter which photos they ended up using, but he did feel slightly down.

"Cheer up," Haruko said. "I like that photo best of all, too. It's the one that really captures Okinawan cats."

"Me too," I chimed in. "I definitely like that one the most."

It would be a pain if Dad moped around, so the two of us teamed up, trying to lift his spirits.

The way we were so in sync, it was like we really had become a mother and son.

The day wasn't too far off, now, when I'd call her *Mom*.

So, not to worry, I said, silently sending out a message to that old cat with the cloudy right eye.

The Night Visitor

Date: –th of ——

In the middle of the night I heard this heavy sniffing sound. Then a brush of whiskers. When I opened my eyes, Tom was stretched on his side, gazing at me.

His black eyes were urging me to *Get up!* Leading the way, turning occasionally to make sure I was following, he led me to the living room cupboard. *I'm hungry, so bring out some snacks!* he was saying. It was 3 a.m.

That damn Tom. Damn, cute Tom.

Date: –th of ——

Getting woken up at 3 a.m. made me sleep-deprived and I decided tonight was the night I would ignore him. I feigned sleep while he sniffed, but then he leaped onto my pillow and walked all over it. I tried not to notice, but that didn't work because then he pretended to accidentally tramp across my face with each fifth step. I gave in and got out of bed.

That damn Tom. Damn, cute Tom.

Date: –th of ——

Yesterday I decided I was definitely not going to get up. My mind made up, I went to bed. I ignored all the sniffing. And Tom retreated.

I was sure tonight I'd be able to get a peaceful night's sleep, when out of nowhere there was this *Pyopyo! Pyopyo!* screeching sound, an electronic bird noise. A toy that screeched like a bird when it was shaken. He was using it as an alarm. He was clearly some kind of genius.

That damn Tom. Damn, cute Tom.

Date: –th of ——

I will not give in. I ignored the sniffing. Ignored the tramping. Ignored all the *pyopyo* racket. He made a temporary retreat.

He leaped onto my pillow once again. Tramping around didn't work anymore, so he straddled my face with all four legs. His belly fur was at the height where it rustled just above my nose, brushing it. Nothing to do but get up.

Date: –th of ——

I will not give in. The sniffing, the trampling, the *pyopyo* noise—consider them ignored. The tummy-fuzz attack I avoided by turning on my side. And Tom retreated. Then from the living room came the crazed bird cry—*Pyopyo! Pyopyo!* ad infinitum. Enraged, he was intentionally making it squawk again and again so I would hear. That insistent angry beat made it impossible to sleep.

That damn Tom. Damn, cute Tom.

Date: –th of ——

I ignored the sniffing, ignored the trampling, and when it came to the *pyopyo* noise I simply grabbed the toy and hid it under the futon covers. I turned away from the tummy fur. Tom stepped over to the opposite side of the pillow, pushed his forehead against mine and twisted it vigorously around. I never imagined he'd try such an outrageously coquettish move. If I ignored it, maybe he wouldn't try it again, I figured. I had to weigh up the pros and cons.

That damn Tom. Damn, cute Tom.

Date: –th of ——

Lack of sleep led to daytime naps. Tom was reclining out in the sun beside the screen door.

Everything seemed so calm when all of a sudden his fur was standing on end and he was making a huge ruckus. I looked through the window and saw we had a cute little visitor.

"My, what a cute little one," I said to the newcomer, and Tom glared up at me with this scary expression on his face. The eyes speak more than the mouth, and his were saying, *What are you talking about, eh?*

That damn Tom. Damn, cute Tom.

After our cute little visitor left, cherry blossom petals began to flutter down against the screen door.

The cherry tree that graced the center of our garden was dropping petals for the first time this spring.

∽

Tom is a cat.

In 2020 the world was besieged by something terrible—not exactly a nuclear firestorm but awful all the same.

For all that, the winter daphne still bloomed, as did the magnolias and the cherry tree.

And next spring they'll bloom again.

And next year, too, Tom and I will continue our nighttime battles.

∽

A year has passed now.

The plum trees have blossomed, but the cherry blossom has yet to appear.

And predictably Tom and I still do battle each and every night.

From behind comes a mysterious, low-frequency humming sound looping over and over.

I look behind me and see that Tom is kneading the boa cushion on the couch, purring all the while, and staring directly at me, his pupils reduced to tiny slits in the sunlight.

What is it? I ask as I come over and bring my face close to his. As he goes on kneading the cushion, he rubs my forehead with his own.

That damn Tom. Damn, cute Tom.

This is all just one big brag, so I don't mind if you forget everything I've said.

Finding Hachi

When he woke up, he was inside a cardboard box.

He looked around and spotted another kitten, a brother born at the same time. White downy fur with a black tail, just like him. There should have been several other siblings alongside him, but it was just him and the one other kitten.

The top of the box had not been closed properly, and light was filtering in through the cracks.

If he meowed, his mother should appear. He mewled a bit, his brother joining in.

Finally, the top of the box opened. It wasn't his mother who was peering in, though, but a child, a boy he'd never seen before. Behind the boy's head was a boundless blue sky. He was gazing silently into the box with a surprised look on his face.

Just then—

"Whoa—cats!" a voice called out. Another boy was now peering inside.

"I wonder why they're here."

"Somebody must have left them."

"Wow—they're so cute!"

The boy who'd just arrived reached out a hand and stroked

the downy fur of both kittens with the tips of his fingers. The first boy followed suit.

"Do you want to pick one up?"

This from the second boy. He scooped up the first kitten in his cupped hands, while the other boy scooped up his brother.

"Do you think somebody wanted to get rid of them?" the second boy asked.

"Probably."

"That's terrible."

"We'd better get going. We'll be late for swimming."

"Yeah, you're right." But they stayed, crouched over the kittens.

The one who lingered the longest was the boy who'd arrived later.

"Come on, Satoru," the first boy said, prodding his friend, and the boy named Satoru reluctantly let his kitten go.

The boys trotted off, the sound of their footsteps fading in the distance.

After a while a shadow loomed over the box. A couple of little girls in yellow hats peered in.

"They're sooo cute!" a voice said from above. A hand abruptly reached inside and lifted the first kitten up. His brother was lifted up, too.

"I wonder if they've been thrown away. The poor things."

"I might take one home."

"Will they let you have a cat in your house?"

"I don't know. But they're so cute. When Mom sees the kitten, I bet she'll let me keep it."

"If you do, let me play with it, okay?"

"Sure! But which one should I take? Which one's cuter?"

The two girls began to compare the kittens. They picked them up, one at a time, and turned them over.

"I think I'll take this one."

"Really? That one? But its tail is bent. It looks weird."

"You think so? Then I'll take this one."

The girl placed the first kitten back in the box and picked up his brother. Unlike his own sharply angled tail, his brother's was perfectly straight.

His brother never came back.

All by himself now, he began to feel lonely and started mewling. Until now if he mewled, the mother cat would make her way quickly over to him, but now she didn't come, no matter how much he called.

The kitten began to grow tired, his mewls weakening. He curled up and started to nod off. He wasn't sure when, but at some point he fell asleep.

He was woken up by two voices shushing each other. He raised his head to see the two boys from before.

"What do you think happened to the other one?"

They seemed to be talking about his brother cat.

"Could we keep this one? How great would that be!"

The boys whispered together, watching him steadily. Finally, the one named Satoru said, as if making a decision, "I'm going to ask my mom."

"Hey, that's not fair!" the other boy exclaimed, and when Satoru flinched at his outburst, he added, "I mean, I'm the one who saw them first."

Satoru apologized. "You're right, you saw them first, Ko-chan, so he's your cat."

Ko-chan picked him up, box and all, and made his way home.

But later—

"A cat? Absolutely not. No. Way!" The man that Ko-chan called Dad wouldn't let the kitten into the house.

After persisting for some time, Ko-chan gave up. Tears sliding down his cheeks, he carried away the box with the kitten. It looked as if it was going to be left outside again, but Ko-chan was heading for Satoru's house.

What's wrong, Ko-chan?"

"Dad said I can't keep the cat," Ko-chan sobbed.

"I get it," Satoru said to his friend. "Leave it to me. I have a great idea!"

As Satoru dragged Ko-chan from the house, a voice called out, asking where he was going.

"Ko-chan and I are going to run away from home for a bit!" he called back.

"I have a plan," Satoru explained to his friend. "I read it in a book at school. A boy found a stray dog, but his father refused to keep it and told him to take it back where he had found it. But the boy didn't want to, so he ran away. His father came looking for him, searching late into the night before he found him. He finally allowed the boy to keep the dog. *But you've got to make sure you take care of him yourself!* his dad told him."

In other words, Ko-chan should do likewise: take the kitten and run away from home. Ko-chan had his doubts, but Satoru was so insistent he finally gave in.

In a nearby park, the two boys sat down for a snack and opened a can of cat food they'd bought at a small supermarket along the way. The kitten was starving and gulped down the tasty, nutritious paste. In his frenzy, he stuck his nose into the paste and gave a sudden sneeze, making Satoru and Ko-chan burst out laughing.

Satoru's plan, though, didn't work out quite as expected.

"Hey!" came the angry voice of Ko-chan's father. "How much longer are you going to sulk, eh? It's about time you called it quits and came home."

"It's the enemy! Run!" Satoru commanded.

The box bumped around as the two of them raced off with it. Inside, the cat was rolling about, no longer able to tell which way was up and which down. After some time, the shaking finally stopped, and the top of the box opened. The two boys peered in, frowning.

"Is he okay? We shook him up a lot."

The kitten couldn't take any more. *Piao!* he howled in protest.

"I heard a cat!" came a voice from below, where a crowd was starting to gather.

"It's coming from the roof!" came another voice. It was Ko-chan's father, growing angry again. "Kosuke, enough!"

Ko-chan began to cry again.

"This isn't working out at all, Satoru. You lied!"

"No, it's too soon to say! We can still pull this off!"

"No, we can't!"

As they started to argue, the people below were discussing how to get hold of the boys.

"I'm going up the fire escape over there."

Ko-chan's father, fueled by anger, started to climb the stairs.

"We're done for!" exclaimed Ko-chan, while Satoru rushed over to the railing on the roof.

What was *done for* wasn't clear, but as long as they didn't shake him around anymore, the kitten didn't care.

Satoru's voice rang out suddenly.

"Don't come any closer! If you do, he'll jump!"

A commotion arose among the crowd below.

". . . is what Ko-chan said!"

"What the—?"

Satoru's announcement wasn't at all what Ko-chan had in

mind. "What are you talking about?" he shouted at Satoru, and the two began arguing again.

"Do you really mean to keep this up, Satoru?!"

"I do, I do. *Hey, he just took off his shoes!*"

A gasp arose again from the people huddled below.

"Stop right now!" It was Ko-chan's father. "Enough of the tantrums. I'm coming up there and dragging you down if I have to."

"Don't do it!" Satoru countered. "Ko-chan's going to jump! Come any further and he's ready to attempt double suicide with the cat!"

The kitten didn't know what *double suicide* meant, but it looked like he was going to be a part of it. And whatever it was, it didn't sound good. *Run for it!* instinct whispered, but the walls of the box were too high for him to scramble over.

As for the two boys, they were bickering again.

"How about not gambling away my life, eh?"

"Look, Ko-chan, you want to keep the cat, don't you?"

"Sure, I do, but still. I mean—shouldn't you first ask your parents to let you keep him at your house?"

"What?" Satoru gulped. "You mean it'll be okay if I keep the cat?"

"Wouldn't most people think of that before coming up with the idea of making their friend kill himself?"

"You should have said so!"

The upshot was that the kitten became Satoru's family cat.

· ·

When he got home, Satoru's parents gave him a piece of their mind.

Satoru listened as he chowed down a plateful of food.

The kitten had his own food, too, which they'd placed in a bowl for him. As he was chewing, the paste-like cat food got steadily pushed into a corner of the bowl and he couldn't quite reach the last few bites. Satoru's mother gathered the pieces with her fingers and held them to his mouth.

The kitten finished his meal and was tidying up around his mouth with his tongue and front paw. Satoru seemed to have finished his meal, too.

"He looks like maybe he's two months old?" Satoru's mother said as she scratched delicately behind the kitten's ears. It felt just like a mother cat licking him, and he couldn't help purring.

"Whoa—he's purring." Satoru, eyes wide, gazed at him.

"They purr when they feel good."

"Really?"

"Here, too," his mother said, stroking under the kitten's chin with her fingertips. Satoru tried it, but his touch was awkward and not as deft.

"He has a hooked tail, doesn't he."

"A hooked tail?"

"The tip is bent like a hook, right?"

Satoru's mother traced the bent end of his tail with her finger. This tail, which bent sharply halfway down, was the reason those girls hadn't chosen him earlier in the day. But here, no one seemed to mind.

"We have to give him a name," the father said, and Satoru's hand shot up.

"I've got it, I've got it!" he shouted. "Lamborghini! Lamborghini!"

"It's too long and hard to say."

"McLaren! McLaren!"

"Something other than car names!"

"But they're cool!"

As Satoru and his mother argued over it, his father interjected.

"I prefer a Japanese name instead of a Western one. He's kind of spotted on his face, so how about *Buchi*—Spot?"

"Nah, that sounds cheesy."

The mother's quick comeback left the father deflated.

Satoru gazed hard at the kitten's face—and then said: "How about Hachi?"

His parents blinked in surprise.

"Look, there's a marking on his forehead like the character *hachi*—eight." (It looks like this: 八.)

"You guys are as bad as each other when it comes to cheesy names," the mother said. "I guess boys take after their fathers." She looked pointedly at Satoru's father and he flinched.

"They may be cheesy names, but Satoru's suggestion has an extra twist to it, since the character *hachi* is a lucky number, the way it spreads out as if gathering in good fortune."

And so it was decided. Holding the kitten with his hands under the front legs, Satoru lifted him up to his face and pressed his nose against his.

"Hachi! Your name is now Hachi! Speak to me, Hachi!"

When the kitten gave a little *meow!* Satoru's face lit up, his cheeks shining.

"He answered! He understands!"

Satoru pressed his cheeks against Hachi's whiskers.

And that's how he became the family's Hachi.

&

Hachi had faintly remembered the home in which the mother cat and his siblings once lived, but after three days at Satoru's, he'd forgotten them completely.

Ko-chan came over almost every day to play. One time he brought a cat teaser toy as a little present.

"My mom bought it for me at the supermarket. It's made with rabbit fur."

Ko-chan waved the toy in front of Hachi, the gray furry part moving wildly from side to side. A hectic back-and-forth for sure, but the movement was too monotonous to be enticing.

"It won't work that way."

Satoru took the cat teaser from Ko-chan and placed the gray furry part under the zabuton cushion, with just the tip of it peeking out. He brought it out for a moment, then hid it, then poked it out again.

Hachi instinctively raised his hips. His bent tail waved and he went into a crouch, his haunches quivering. Then he pounced and held down the toy with his front paws. Just when he thought he had it, the cat teaser slipped from his paws and wiggled away.

He pounced again, but the toy had slipped under the cushion and vanished. But then it peeped out at the other end of the cushion, and Hachi, enthralled, dodged and pounced again. He'd almost grabbed it, but it eluded his grasp, and he couldn't quite get hold of it.

Ko-chan sighed in admiration.

"Boy, you're good, Satoru."

"He-he!" Satoru laughed.

He was proud of his skill with the cat teaser, though it was his mother who'd shown him how. She was even better at it. She'd had cats, she said, when she was a child.

"I get how to do it. Let me try," said Ko-chan.

He copied Satoru, moving the cat teaser toy around, but he moved it too quickly. Hachi's eyes swiveled around, watching the toy, but he couldn't time his leaps to grab it.

"Move it more slowly."

"Is Hachi maybe a bit slow?"

"No, what Hachi is is laid-back."

Laid-back was the way Satoru's parents had put it. It meant something like *slow* but was a kinder way of saying it.

Ko-chan made the tip of the cat teaser pop out from under the sofa, then disappear. This was easier for Hachi to catch.

..

S nack time, boys—"

Satoru's mother brought in warm steamed buns. Momentarily distracted, Ko-chan slowed down the game and, spotting his chance, Hachi made a lunge, snagging the fur toy in his paws. He began to chew on it, carefully working from the base upward.

"Did you put raisins in the buns?"

"Not this time. I don't always."

"Oh," Satoru wailed, pouting, and his mother flicked a finger against his forehead.

"No complaints," she said.

"I like the chocolate-flavored ones." This from Ko-chan.

"We've run out of cocoa powder, I'm afraid. Just eat what's put in front of you—"

Ko-chan got his own forehead flick. He seemed happy to receive it, though.

Deep into their snacks, the boys ignored the cat teaser, so Hachi took a flying leap at Satoru's fingertips and started chewing on them instead.

"Ouch! Stop it!"

But Hachi was determined to catch the flying fingertips. "Okay, okay, I get it," Satoru said. He rummaged around in the cloth box containing Hachi's toys and took out a toy mouse with white fur and a skinny leather tail.

"You like this, don't you?" Satoru held the leather tail and swung the mouse around. "Go get it!" he yelled and tossed it down the hall. Hachi scrambled after it, skidding on his way. Once the mouse was trapped, he pushed it down the polished hallway.

"Hachi really likes that mouse."

"It will keep him busy for a while."

"Do you think he could catch a real mouse?"

"I wonder."

A couple of months later Ko-chan's question was answered. *"Eeee—a mouse!"* his mother screamed as she was tidying up inside a cupboard. She'd just opened the storage space above it when a mouse had dashed out.

It sped across the room and ran straight at Hachi.

"Go on. Grab it, Hachi!"

All well and good, but this mouse was three times the size of his white toy mouse. And it was a dirty gray. Above all, though, it ran around on its own without being pushed or slapped.

Unsure what to do, Hachi instinctively edged away.

The mouse hurtled right between Hachi's legs, toward the front door. Shocked by the sensation of the mouse racing under him, Hachi plunked his belly down on the floor.

"Let's chase him outside!" Satoru's father yelled, striding to the front door with a rolled-up newspaper clutched in his hand.

"Satoru, close the door!" his mother called. Satoru pulled

the door from the living room to the hallway shut, and crouched down in front of Hachi.

"You're a cat, but you lost out to a mouse. That's pathetic."

For Hachi this was withering criticism. But this wasn't the kind of mouse that Hachi was familiar with.

"I suppose it was the first-ever mouse you've seen, Hachi. You've led a pretty sheltered life, haven't you?"

I'm telling you, that was no mouse, Hachi meowed in protest, but neither Satoru nor his mother paid any attention.

"Hey, I chased it out of the house, guys," Satoru's father said. "That mouse tunneled right under you, didn't he, Hachi?" He stroked Hachi's head consolingly.

But that was no mouse! Hachi wanted to say, but who would listen?

"Even when mice appear in our house, our cat's no help at all."

Just ignore them, Hachi said to himself as he curled up at one end of the sofa. *They don't get it, so take no notice.*

"It's okay. We don't have a cat, we have Hachi."

"Are you upset, Hachi?"

Satoru came over and tickled his belly. A little late in the day, it seemed to Hachi.

"It's okay that you can't catch mice, Hachi. Because you're our family's darling cat."

Hachi planned to sulk for a while, but with all the scratching behind his ears and stroking under his chin by Satoru, he was overcome and before long started purring.

⤎

When Hachi was first brought home, Satoru had been a big boy, but before he knew it, Satoru had become more of a child than him.

Cat time and human time seemed to move at a different pace. Around the moment he realized that cat time moved more quickly, Hachi had passed Satoru and was already a fully grown adult.

The cat teaser and toy mouse didn't excite him as much as they had when he was a kitten. Whenever Satoru tried to get him to play, he couldn't always be bothered.

"And he was so, so tiny when we first got him."

Back then, he'd fit snugly into Ko-chan's cupped hands; he'd been no bigger than the size of a fist, Satoru commented.

He must have been a bit bigger than that, but Satoru seemed to like to emphasize how small Hachi had been. Memories of when he was a kitten must have been deeply etched into his mind. From Hachi's perspective, when he was a kitten Satoru had loomed over him like a small mountain.

Compared with Hachi, Satoru and Ko-chan were growing up quite slowly. In the space of a year, a young cat would grow many times larger than its kitten size, but for the boys, after a year, they had still only grown an inch or two.

How many years are they planning to take before they are grown up? Hachi wondered, finding it all extremely puzzling.

..

Spring arrived, the second since the boys had found him.

The school backpacks the boys carried were starting to look tight on them. Hachi hadn't noticed it on a daily basis, but suddenly he realized how their arms and legs had sprouted.

Spring passed and early summer arrived, and Satoru came home with a golden trophy. He'd brought home a few over the last few years, but never one this big.

Dinner that night consisted of all Satoru's favorite foods. *Kara-age* chicken nuggets and potato salad, plus takeaway assorted sushi, minus the wasabi, and nigiri sushi topped with omelet strips.

Hachi, too, was given a feast—a large bowl of steamed chicken breast.

As the family sat down to their meal, they made a toast, Satoru with orange juice, his father and mother with beer.

"Congratulations, Satoru, on winning!"

He'd apparently taken part in a big competition at the swimming club he and Ko-chan attended. It was the biggest swimming competition he'd ever competed in, and Satoru had come first.

"You're amazing, Satoru," his father said. "When I was at elementary school, the furthest I could swim was twenty-five meters."

"It makes sense," his mother said, "given that we grew up in Hokkaido."

From what Satoru's mother said, the oceans and rivers in

Hokkaido were so cold that there were few opportunities to swim, even in the summer, and not many people from Hokkaido were therefore able to swim.

"The swimming coach said he hopes you carry on when you go to junior high. Will you, do you think?"

Happily chewing on his mother's *kara-age*, Satoru looked a little dazed. He'd had three large nuggets already, with some nigiri sushi in between.

"Mmm . . . if Ko-chan does, too," he answered absently, biting down on his fourth chicken nugget. For his part, Ko-chan didn't seem to be that keen on swimming. He was among the cheerleaders at today's competition.

"There's a swimming team in junior high, isn't there?" Satoru's father said, trying to arouse his son's interest, but again Satoru just said, "If Ko-chan does," before digging into the nigiri sushi.

"Did Ko-chan say he would?"

"He's not sure yet."

For Satoru, the appeal of swimming seemed to boil down to a question of whether he could be together with Ko-chan.

His father seemed disappointed that Satoru wasn't more enthusiastic.

"Well, Satoru should carry on if he wants to," he said, before pestering his wife to bring another bottle of beer. "Keeper of the Purse Strings, if you would be so kind!" he pleaded, and his wife smiled and went through to the kitchen.

Having had his fill of nigiri sushi, Satoru helped himself to a tuna roll. Hachi scratched at his sleeve and Satoru peeled off a slice of tuna and handed it to him, leaving just the sushi rice for himself.

It wasn't clear if Satoru and Ko-chan would carry on swimming in junior high, but Hachi knew one thing for sure: he would keep watch over these two boys as they continued to grow.

He and his brother had been abandoned, and he'd ended up in this home, over all others. This had to be so he could watch over Satoru and Ko-chan as they edged toward adulthood.

"Hachi—"

Tired after his big meal, perhaps, Satoru rested his fingers on Hachi's tail. Satoru liked the cat's hooked tail and enjoyed playing with it.

The little girl who'd picked his brother to take home had left Hachi behind because of this bent tail. But it was this crooked tail that turned out to be Hachi's saving grace.

ভ

The sauna-like heat of summer had passed, and the wind was finally growing cooler.

On a cloudless autumn day, the sky looked so high.

"Mom? What about my bag? You said you'd buy it for me today!"

Satoru was back from school, and pestering his mother.

"All right, all right . . ."

Laughing, his mother fetched the travel bag she'd bought earlier in the day, a big blue bag made of a crinkly fabric.

"Can I start packing?"

"But your school trip isn't for another week."

"But if I get ready early, I won't have to rush later on!"

The upcoming school trip to Kyoto was a major event for Satoru.

"I need three days' worth of clothes, so how many pairs of underpants should I take?"

"Two, I would think."

"Not three?"

"The first day's pair you'll be wearing when you leave, won't you?"

"But will that be enough?"

"Then why not take three pairs? If you wet your bed, you'll be in trouble."

His mother said this teasingly, and Satoru went red. "I don't do that anymore!" he insisted, slapping her arm in protest. "I haven't done that for years!"

Satoru was right. Hachi had still been a kitten when Satoru had drawn a world map on his bedding. Back then Hachi, too, had had some toilet mishaps of his own. Ancient memories that were fading away now.

But now Hachi had no more toilet accidents, and neither did Satoru.

"I'm not going to wet the bed, but it feels like two's not enough."

"Then why don't you ask Ko-chan?"

When Ko-chan came over, Satoru asked him how many pairs of underpants he planned to take for the three days. He drew pictures of underpants in a sketchbook as they discussed the matter.

"The first day we'll take a bath so that's the first pair. After the second day's bath, that's two. And the third day . . ."

"The third day we'll be coming home, so we won't need another pair."

Ko-chan was in the two-pair camp, to which Satoru countered, "But we're going for three days," though he didn't sound so confident anymore. In fine lines, he drew several pairs of underpants in a corner of the sketchbook.

"Here's why—" his mother cut in as she passed by. She took the pencil from Satoru and drew a figure with underpants on and wearing a baseball cap. "You'll have one pair to start off with, the underpants you'll be wearing when you leave here. Then the pair you'll change into after your bath on the first day, and the pair you'll change into after the bath on the second day. See? That makes three pairs altogether."

His mother pointed at each pair in the sketchbook, counting them, and the two boys finally seemed convinced.

"So we'll only need to take two pairs!"

"That's right," his mother replied, beaming, but when she got to the kitchen, she paused. "Wait a second!" She was reading the handout for the trip that was taped to the fridge. "I'm sorry, boys! The guidelines for the trip say to take an extra pair! So it's three pairs after all!"

"*What?!*"

The boys were none too happy to find the decision overturned.

"Okay—so three days' worth of underpants comes to how many pairs?" said Satoru.

"Basically two pairs. *Basically*."

His mother came over, took the pencil and next to the second day's pair of underpants drew, in parentheses, another pair.

"You're taking one more pair, just in case."

"Just in case?"

"Like I said, if you wet the bed, for instance . . ."

"*I don't wet the bed!!*"

After all the fuss, they finally settled on three pairs.

"What about socks? Three pairs, too?" Satoru asked, and his mother went to the fridge again to check the guidelines.

"It doesn't say anything about extra socks. Two should be enough, I would think."

"But what if it rains hard and they get wet?"

"If you're so worried, take three pairs."

Satoru and Ko-chan launched into another discussion.

Cats get by just the way they are, but humans can have it tough. With one ear twitching at the boys, Hachi stepped inside the wide-open travel bag and curled up.

. .

The day of the school trip loomed.

"So next is . . . a toothbrush!"

"Check!"

Satoru and Ko-chan brought out their toothbrush sets from their bags and held them up like *inro*, the small cases that hang from the *obi*, or belt of a kimono. Ko-chan had lugged his travel bag all the way over to Satoru's so they could go through the checklist together the day before the trip.

Ko-chan read it aloud, and they extracted each item from their bags in turn, showing each other.

"You sure you want to take everything out like that?" Satoru's mother called as she took in the laundry.

"We're good to go," the boys called back, not really listening.

"Underpants?"

"Three pairs!"

"Socks?"

"Two pairs!"

They'd apparently settled on two pairs.

Satisfied, they zipped up their bags. Behind Ko-chan lay his toothbrush set, left out in all the excitement.

Look what happened. Hachi rolled his body over the toothbrush set a bit.

"Hey! Ko-chan—you forgot your toothbrush!" Satoru called out.

"Oh, my gosh!" Ko-chan said and grabbed the toothbrush

from Hachi. "You shouldn't play with that, Hachi. It's not a toy."

I showed you it's missing and that's how you react? That's not nice. Hachi narrowed his eyes.

"Let's play with something else," suggested Satoru quickly, and he brought over the cat teaser toy.

Hachi was still a little put out but decided that, with the boys away for three days, if they thought he was upset when they left him, they'd worry about him on their trip, so he should cut them some slack. When all was said and done, Satoru and Ko-chan were still children, and you couldn't expect them to be totally considerate.

Not to mention how enticing the cat teaser toy was when Satoru wielded it, the way his mother had shown him.

Hachi bounded boisterously after the toy as it sped away, then he came to an abrupt stop, keeping a close eye on it as it leaped around. Ko-chan took over a few times, but his handling of the cat teaser was, as always, not as deft as Satoru's. He never let Hachi catch it, for one thing, which made it boring.

"It's almost time for dinner," Satoru's mother called from the kitchen. "You should go home soon, Ko-chan," she added, "since the trip is tomorrow. You're all meeting up pretty early in the morning."

"Do I have to? But Hachi's in such a good mood."

Ahh—no need to worry. I'm good, Hachi thought. He let go

of the cat teaser and Satoru's mother added, "You can play with Hachi anytime."

"Okaay—"

"See you," Ko-chan said to Hachi, stroking the top of his head, and he left, lugging his travel bag with him. Once Satoru had waved Ko-chan through the front door, he sorted out his own bag. Neither one of the boys had noticed Hachi stepping over their things and sniffing to ensure they still hadn't left anything behind. They were, after all, still children.

That evening while they were having dinner, Satoru was feeling excited.

"So, Dad, what souvenir would you like me to bring back for you?"

"I'll be happy with anything as long as you choose it."

His father was trying to please him, but Satoru shot back, *"Boooring!"* and his father looked dejected.

"What about you, Mom?"

"I'd like some Yojiya facial blotting paper."

"Facial blotting paper?"

His mother stood up and fetched her shopping tote bag. She opened up a little pouch where she kept her powder compact and lipstick and took out a small folder full of translucent sheets of paper.

"Here, this is what I mean. The Yojiya brand has a drawing of a woman's face on the outside."

"What does it look like?"

"Well . . ."

On a memo pad, his mother drew him a face like that of a crude but charming *kokeshi* doll. Satoru studied the drawing.

"If there's a different, cuter brand, is it okay if I buy that?"

"No, it has to be the Yojiya brand," his mother insisted.

"I guess I have no choice, then," Satoru said, nodding seriously.

That night Satoru was so worked up he couldn't sleep. He kept turning over, and every time he did, Hachi had to find a new spot on the bed.

"What should I do? I have to get up so early tomorrow . . ."

Satoru picked up his bedside clock to see the time and seemed about to burst into tears. Finally he threw back the covers and got up. Worriedly, Hachi padded silently behind as Satoru left his bedroom and headed for the living room. The light was still on, his mother still up.

"Mom . . ."

"Okay, I get it." His mother smiled and stood up. She'd been writing something at the table but now went into the kitchen. Satoru heard her moving about and the ding of the microwave, out of which emerged a steaming mug, the scent of hot milk wafting from it.

This was the *special sleep medicine* his mother made for him the night before a school outing or family trip.

"Today's drink is special, with two teaspoons of honey. That should do the trick."

Satoru nodded and sat down on the sofa, blowing on the hot milk to cool it down.

"Mom, have you ever been to Kyoto?"

"Many times."

"Did you go to Kiyomizu Temple?"

"I did, yes. The boiled tofu there was delicious. If you have time on the trip, you should try some."

"Tofu? Boring!"

Satoru sipped at his milk as they chatted, and finally his eyelids started to droop.

"'Night, Mom," he said, and headed back to his room. He rolled over a few times before finally falling fast asleep. Hachi waited before moving toward his feet and curling himself up.

The next morning, Ko-chan came to fetch him and he got up on time and set off happily with his friend.

Two days later, he would be back home with all his souvenirs.

At least that was the plan.

∾

The day after Satoru left, it didn't stop raining.

And naturally Hachi felt his eyelids grow heavy, for rain always made cats sleepy.

Hachi had just eaten his breakfast and had curled up on the sofa when Satoru's father came over and looked out the window as he fastened his necktie.

"Wow, it's really coming down. Do you think Satoru will be okay?"

"The weather report says it'll be clear in western Japan," his wife replied.

"I hope so. If it's raining like this over there, it will spoil their trip. I'm going to get soaked just walking to the station."

"Don't worry, I'll drive you."

After he'd eaten, Satoru's father put on his suit jacket while his mother took the plates to the kitchen and left them to soak.

And then the two of them hurried out. "See you later!" Satoru's father called to Hachi. His wife didn't say anything. She planned to come right back.

The disheartening sound of falling rain didn't seem to let up. Cats spent rainy days like this fast asleep. Pouring rain, *zaa zaa*. Dozing cat, *zzz zzz*. Pouring rain, dozing cat, *zaa zaa, zzz zzz*.

At some point, amid the unceasing rain, Hachi's ears twitched, as he thought he heard a muted siren far off, though he could have been imagining it.

Finally he'd had enough of sleeping. He gave a wide yawn and dropped his back in a downward cat stretch, then leaped down from the sofa and padded gracefully toward the kitchen. His stomach was telling him it must be lunchtime.

In his little food bowl, in its usual spot next to the sink, there were a few crunchy leftovers from breakfast. Not enough to fill him up, but he went ahead and ate them. Satoru's mother would soon notice and refill the bowl.

But even after he had licked the bowl clean, she didn't

appear in the kitchen. The house was filled with the sound of rainfall, but no sign of Satoru's mother moving around elsewhere in the house.

Hachi wondered what was going on, but, unable to fight the heaviness in his eyes that crept up on him, he curled up and went to sleep.

Zaaa zaaa, zzz zzz, zaa zaa, zzz zzz, zzz zzz, zzz zzz.

Before he realized it, the sound of the rain had begun to slacken off. His ears twitched at the clatter of the key in the front door.

You're so late—do you have any idea how hungry I am? But when Hachi strolled over to the front door, it wasn't Satoru's mother. The face of the woman slightly resembled her but looked a lot younger.

This was Satoru's aunt, his mother's younger sister. She was always visiting.

The aunt gave a small flinch when she spotted Hachi. He was aware from past experience that she seemed uneasy around cats, so he didn't venture any closer.

"Satoru."

Urged on by his aunt, Satoru appeared at the entrance lugging his travel bag.

Hachi was about to welcome him back by brushing against his knees, but instead he froze just inside the door—

Was this really Satoru?

The boy's face was pale, expressionless.

His face usually flitted rapidly from one expression to another, but now it had set into just one, his eyes wide open and his mouth tight shut.

"Change into these clothes," the aunt instructed, handing him a paper bag. Satoru awkwardly reached out and took it. You could almost hear his joints squeaking as he moved, like some unoiled machine.

Hachi waited a moment, then followed him as he headed to his room. This didn't seem like Satoru at all and his fur began to prick up in mild fright, yet he wasn't about to leave him on his own when he was looking like that.

Inside the paper bag his aunt had given him was a suit like the one his father was always wearing. Except for the shirt, all the clothes were black—the jacket, the trousers and the tie. Even the socks were black.

Satoru tugged off his colorful sweatshirt and put on the close-fitting white shirt. He pulled on the trousers and jacket and snapped on the clip-on tie.

Finally, he exchanged his red-striped socks for the black ones. He threw the red-striped socks on top of his sweatshirt. Then, all of a sudden, he began to hurl himself around the room. He kicked at the sweatshirt and sent it flying. The red socks on top took off in another direction.

Hachi scampered under the bed, belly low. Usually Satoru would quickly apologize if he startled the cat. But not this time. He completely ignored him.

Face blank, Satoru stamped on the sweatshirt over and over again. Soundlessly, but no less violently, he continued to abuse the sweatshirt. As if it were to blame for everything.

Someone knocked at the door.

"Satoru, are you ready?"

At the sound of his aunt Noriko's voice, Satoru suddenly stopped stamping on the sweatshirt and left the room calmly as if nothing had happened.

His aunt was dressed from head to foot in black.

"Let's go to where your father and mother are."

Satoru nodded and started walking behind her. Hachi paused before setting off behind them.

Satoru was slipping on his shoes when he ran back inside as if he'd forgotten something. He was heading for the kitchen. He poured a mountain of crunchy cat food into Hachi's bowl and changed his water.

Then he made his way to the bathroom, where he cleaned up Hachi's litter tray and poured in a bit more sand.

Even though his face was expressionless, and even though he'd silently tortured his sweatshirt, Satoru was still Satoru. Hachi rubbed the top of his head against Satoru's knees. Satoru didn't say anything, his face remained blank, but he did scratch Hachi's ears a little.

Hachi saw Satoru and his aunt off. As the front door shut behind them, he heard the sound of their footsteps receding. He had no idea where they had gone, but he did know it was somewhere sad.

. .

Satoru had forgotten to turn on the lights, and the house eventually grew pitch-black. Hachi ate his cat food in the dark, lapped a little water and spent the rest of the time napping or looking out the window.

It was late at night when Satoru returned with his aunt.

When Hachi padded to the front door, Satoru seemed to shudder at how dark it was inside. His aunt went in first, switching on the lights, and finally Satoru took off his shoes and walked in.

The aunt went around turning on the lights in the hallway, the living room and the kitchen. Satoru followed as the lights came on. In the kitchen he saw that half of the cat food was left.

Satoru and his aunt took turns taking a shower and went to bed without eating. Satoru slept in his own room, while his aunt spread out a futon in the living room.

Hachi slid into Satoru's room, where the crumpled, mistreated sweatshirt still lay.

Satoru had gone to bed, but when Hachi landed beside him by his pillow, he found him wide awake, staring, his eyes like vacant dark holes, at the light from the small lightbulb.

Satoru moved his pillow aside to make room for Hachi, but Hachi heard no gentle snoring coming from him as he usually did. Hachi fell asleep first, so he had no idea when those vacant eyes of Satoru's finally did close.

The next morning was bright and sunny, brilliant sunlight streaming in through the gaps in the curtains.

Satoru and his aunt again changed into their black clothes and left, but not before Satoru had filled Hachi's food bowl to overflowing and left the light on in the living room.

Hachi thought they'd come back late that day, as before, but it was different this time.

As the sun was setting, from outside the house came a loud voice, like a howling animal. And gradually, inescapably, the voice grew more shrill, echoing louder and louder against the walls.

Hachi sat at the entrance, ready to greet it.

It was Ko-chan who opened the door. As he walked in, he was propping up the wailing Satoru.

He stumbled slowly toward the living room. An animal howl rang from him. He sat down, shoulders heaving.

Ko-chan might have helped him home, but he had no idea what to do now. He stood wavering beside Satoru.

In a single leap, Hachi was on Satoru's lap. Satoru rested his palm on Hachi's cheek, and Hachi licked his hand carefully, very carefully.

It's okay. It's okay.

I'm here. I'm here.

He carried on licking his hand, and finally, as if worn-out, Satoru's howls began to subside.

∽

Father and mother came back home inside two identical white urns.

Satoru had been taken in by his aunt and was moving house.

"But you'll take Hachi with you, won't you?" Ko-chan sounded like he was praying this would be the case. "If Hachi's with you . . . even in your new home you won't be alone, Satoru. You won't be as lonely."

"I can't take Hachi with me. 'Cause my aunt is transferred around a lot with her work."

Satoru seemed to have resigned himself to it long ago. But it was painful for him to have to say so to Ko-chan.

"Then what about Hachi?"

"Some other relatives of mine said they'd take him."

"Do you know these relatives well, Satoru?"

Satoru shook his head. Ko-chan bit his lip.

"I—I'm going to go see if we can keep Hachi at our house!" Ko-chan called as he left, but after dark he was back, clearly having cried his eyes out.

"Dad said no way."

From his thick, swollen eyelids it was obvious how bravely Ko-chan must have battled to convince him.

"It's okay," Satoru said, his tearful face smiling. "I'm happy that you tried."

The two of them wept silently as they stroked Hachi, and Hachi let them stroke him as much as they wanted.

He'd been so sure he'd stay in this house and watch over the two boys as they grew up. But for both children and cats, life never seemed to turn out the way you wanted.

Later, an older man, an uncle of Satoru's, came to collect

Hachi. He was tall, with a deeply lined face, and when he smiled, his eyes disappeared into the wrinkles around them.

Satoru was in the living room, his arms tight around Hachi's belly. The man tousled Satoru's hair.

"Don't worry about a thing. Everyone in our family loves cats. We'll take good care of him, don't you worry."

Satoru's face lit up. It was the first time since his parents had disappeared into those two white urns that he'd looked like that.

"Be sure to make Hachi happy."

"Leave it to me," the man said.

Even so, when it came time to say goodbye, Satoru blubbered as if his tear ducts were broken.

"I wonder if there's really no way Noriko-chan can take him."

The man said this out of pity for Satoru, but his aunt's current place didn't allow pets, apparently.

"Look, let the last thing Hachi sees from you be a smile, or he'll worry about you," the man said, and Satoru tried to smile through his tears. He forced the corners of his lips up into a smile, even if it was a bit lopsided and weird-looking.

"Hachi, take care!" Satoru called out, giving a big wave.

That was the last Hachi ever saw of him.

∽

For about three hours, Hachi swayed back and forth in his carrier before they finally arrived at the uncle's house, where there were four children.

The eldest boy was even taller than his father. Next was a girl, then a boy, and another boy, each progressively smaller, the youngest about the same age as Satoru.

Which is perhaps why the first name Hachi remembered belonged to this youngest boy. He was named Tsutomu. Like Satoru, his expression changed by the minute. He didn't go swimming but was into baseball.

And he fought with his elder brothers and sister every day. Being the smallest, he always came off worst, whether it be grappling with them, or arguing. Hachi's daily routine included sidling up to him as he cried, and licking his hands and knees. Tsutomu lost every day, so blubbering was an everyday occurrence.

"Usually cats get most attached to the person who feeds them." Both the uncle and aunt found it odd that Hachi would favor Tsutomu over anybody else.

"Hachi is sorry for Tsutomu since he's such a wimp," Tsutomu's sister said with a burst of laughter. When they argued, she was the one who most often made Tsutomu cry.

"Shut up!" Tsutomu yelled and gave her a swift kick from behind.

"Now you're for it!" she yelled and chased after him.

He'd end up crying no matter what, so why the boy would get involved with her was a complete mystery to Hachi.

"Hachi doesn't seem to like going out much." The aunt seemed to find this odd. "When I clean the flat and open the window, he'll go out into the garden, but that's about it. With our apartment being on the first floor, he should go out for a little stroll at least."

"Maybe he was an indoor cat at his previous place?" the uncle said.

"The poor thing," the aunt replied, frowning slightly.

"I wouldn't say that," their eldest son chimed in. "People are afraid of accidents and things, so there are more and more homes that keep their cats indoors all the time."

"Well, our little Milk was in an accident, too, wasn't he," the boy next in age piped up.

Milk was the name of the very first cat this family had had. The sister had named the cat, though the boys found the name too cutesy and hadn't been very fond of him as a result.

"Hachi's a bit slow. Maybe it's good he doesn't want to go outside."

His sister gently poked Hachi's cheek with her forefinger.

"Stop it!" It was Tsutomu who broke in. "He's not slow. He's just laid-back!"

Hearing Tsutomu speak, Hachi recalled another boy the same age.

No, what Hachi is is laid-back.

It was Satoru who had rephrased *slow* as *laid-back*.

Hachi looked up to see a child smiling down at him, using the same words as Satoru as he scratched him behind his ear.

Ah—I get it, Hachi thought.

My job now is to watch over Tsutomu in this place as he grows.

Satoru and Tsutomu are the same age. They use the same gentle words. As Tsutomu gets bigger, so will Satoru.

Tsutomu replaced Satoru in his mind, naturally, and that was that.

It did bother him that he had left Satoru, but he was finally able to feel at home here.

Tsutomu tickled his throat with his fingers, and for the first time since he'd arrived in this new family, Hachi purred to his heart's content.

～

Spring followed winter and the cherry blossoms were out. Tsutomu now wore a school jacket with a stand-up collar and had started going to junior high.

As before, he continued playing baseball. When had he stopped swimming? Hachi wondered. Doing both was hard, so it couldn't be helped. Seemed he'd put away that golden trophy somewhere.

He played sports every day and ate loads. He shot up in height, too. It was hard to believe there used to be a time when he had grown so slowly each year, since the following year, he shot up all of four inches.

Their baseball practice always seemed to be outside, and his skin became so dark it looked like it was boiled in soy sauce.

"When the light is behind him," the aunt said, "his face is so dark I can't tell where his eyes and nose are!"

"He's even darker than me. Imagine that!" the uncle added with a laugh.

As always, though, Tsutomu's expression changed by the minute. And the fights with his elder brothers and sister never let up. But the quarrels with his sister were more verbal now than physical. His sister's sharp tongue had become even sharper, incorrigible. Tsutomu no longer burst into tears when they fought, though on occasion a few did well up in his eyes.

Hachi loved Tsutomu, beaten to the punch by his sister, and teary-eyed. He loved all of them—the uncle, the aunt, the eldest brother, the second-eldest brother and the sister—but he loved Tsutomu most of all.

When Hachi ran, his hind legs got all tangled up, but Tsutomu was nice enough to call him *laid-back*. When Hachi had come across a mouse for the first time in his life and stood there, frozen, wasn't he the one who'd said, "It's okay that you can't catch mice, Hachi. Because you're our family's darling cat"?

He told anyone who wiggled the cat teaser toy too fast to *Move it more slowly*. Now, what was that boy's name again? Who was he? Tsutomu's friend. He'd come over to play every day, a long, long time ago, when Hachi was still just a kitten. When had he stopped coming?

Cat time passed fast. The time when he was a kitten was so long ago it was like back before he was born.

He couldn't remember the boy's name. Even so, he must be okay somewhere. *I mean, look at how much Tsutomu's arms and legs have shot out.*

Please, let them all be well, and happy.

Spring came around once more, and the eldest brother left home. He had passed his entrance exam to college and would be living in the city.

The apartment grew a bit quieter. The absence of the eldest brother was one reason, but the other children's quarrels had grown slightly less boisterous. Tsutomu and the second-eldest brother would occasionally tussle, but that was about it.

Tsutomu's arms and legs grew even longer because he got a daily workout at baseball practice and packed away so much food every day.

In the summer baseball tournament, his team got as far as the semifinals. Tsutomu came home crying tears of regret.

"Isn't making the semifinals good enough?" his mother said, and his sister chimed in with, "That's right. You can try again when you're in high school."

"Shut up!" Tsutomu yelled, losing his temper. "This is the only time I'll play with these teammates!"

"Hey, I'm only trying to make you feel better," his sister shot back and threw a cushion at him.

I don't think you should have reacted that way, Tsutomu, Hachi thought, rubbing his side up against the boy's knees. As Tsutomu gave the cat a soft stroke, he gradually calmed down. Later, he apologized to his sister.

"But making it to the semifinals is still quite an accomplishment," his mother said, and she ordered takeaway sushi for dinner. To which she added her own chicken nuggets and potato salad—his favorite meal since he was little.

The exact same menu as they'd eaten when he first won the swimming competition, Hachi seemed to recall.

But now he didn't seem to like nigiri sushi that much. Tsutomu ate only the tuna. When Hachi tugged at his sleeve, he carefully scraped off the wasabi from a piece of tuna sushi, gave it to Hachi and swallowed down the sushi rice in a single gulp.

"Are you going to keep playing baseball in high school?" his father asked, to which Tsutomu grunted a yes.

"Didn't you say you didn't want to unless you could play with the friends you're with now?" His sister still seemed to be holding a grudge against him for snapping at her when she'd only been trying to cheer him up.

"I'm not that childish. And a few of them will be going to the same high school as me."

"*Stop it*, all of you!" their mother shouted, and they reluctantly simmered down.

My gosh—they've all grown so big, but at heart they're still just kids, Hachi thought. *How big do humans have to get, anyway, before they're grown up?*

As for Hachi, he had only faint memories of the days when he was a kitten.

Your name is now Hachi! Was that Tsutomu who'd said that, pressing his cheek against his? And scooped him out of his box? No—that's not how it was. The uncle had brought him to this apartment in a carrier. Okay, then, what about that memory of being in a cardboard box? Of being in the box for a long time, and being shaken around and feeling queasy?

Why had he been shaken around so much? They wouldn't let him keep Hachi, so the boy pretended to run away from home, but it didn't work out and they had started arguing—

This isn't working out at all. You lied!

Look, you want to keep the cat, don't you?!

I mean—shouldn't you first ask your parents to let you keep him at your house?

So who was it that was being criticized when things didn't work out?

Tsutomu? Tsutomu played baseball. When did he quit swimming? *If ——chan does it with me. But if ——chan doesn't . . .*

"Hachi, how about some tuna?"

The sister waved a piece of tuna held between chopsticks. *Well, if she's going to the trouble, how can I refuse?* Hachi thought. She was holding the tuna up pretty high, so Hachi stood on his hind legs and gave it a good sniff. But his mouth wouldn't quite reach, and he lost his balance and ended up falling back onto his bottom.

"Ha ha! You're so slow."

"He's *laid-back*, not slow. Don't tease him like that."

Tsutomu grabbed the slice of tuna from his sister's chopsticks. Bending down, using his palm as a plate, he held out the tuna for Hachi.

"But the way he's so slow is cute."

"What an awful girl she is, right, Hachi?"

As before, Tsutomu had gently rephrased the word *slow* as *laid-back*. Being called *laid-back* was something Hachi had grown used to from a long time ago.

"Does it taste good?"

Hachi tipped his head sideways and licked the tuna in Tsutomu's hand.

The way time moved was certainly different for cats and humans. It was much faster for cats. When had he first realized this?

Tsutomu had grown much bigger, but was apparently still not an adult. Before he became one, he had to get through a test called a high school entrance exam, so in the autumn and winter all he did was study, study, study.

At New Year, a man came to visit; he had a beard like a bear's.

"How've you been, Hachi?" he asked, but when he bent to pick him up, Hachi flinched.

"What the—? Have you forgotten me? Even though you saw me during the summer break, too?"

"You were only back for a week, and a cat's little brain forgets. Plus you've now grown that beard."

Hearing the aunt and the man talking, Hachi finally realized this was the eldest son.

I'm sorry, I should have recognized you sooner, Hachi thought. To apologize, he rubbed himself up against the eldest brother's knees, and the brother, having regained his good humor, pulled Hachi onto his chest. When he rubbed his cheek against Hachi's whiskers, the beard scratched, and Hachi thrust his legs into the brother's chest and scampered off.

Tsutomu spent New Year with his nose in his books and passed his exam. When the single cherry tree in the garden began to blossom, he swapped his jacket with the stand-up collar for a blazer and started at his new school.

He immediately joined the baseball team and came back every day covered in mud. His new school apparently had a strong baseball team, and the practice schedule was intense.

The cherry blossoms scattered, and all that was left on the tree were the leaves. Caterpillars were plopping down from the branches. Every year at this time, the aunt and sister insisted that they cut the tree down—that's how much they hated caterpillars.

"What are you talking about? It's a symbol, this tree." This was the uncle's line every year as he soothed the female contingent.

On one occasion, Tsutomu had come into the apartment with a caterpillar perched on his shoulder and the aunt and sister had screamed until the doors shook.

Another day, a caterpillar had somehow crawled into the hallway. When the aunt and sister spotted it, they went berserk.

Thinking he'd get rid of it for them, Hachi gave it a couple of good whacks with his front paw.

A burning pain shot through his paw pads. When he screeched, it was Tsutomu who raced to his side.

"Hachi, what's wrong?"

Tsutomu figured out at a glance what had happened.

"Did the caterpillar sting you?"

"No way! You mean the caterpillars from the cherry tree? They sting?" His sister raised a ruckus, and the second-eldest brother answered her.

"Most of them don't sting, but some of them do."

"Ugh! Get rid of it! *Get rid of it!*"

While the second-eldest brother removed the caterpillar, Tsutomu knelt down to apply disinfectant to Hachi's paw.

"Maybe I should put on some cream for insect bites, too?" he asked his mother.

"It would be better not to," she declaimed, like an oracle. "Because he might lick it. If it swells up, I'll take him to the vet tomorrow."

The second-eldest brother came back in, having disposed of the caterpillar, and gave Hachi's head a gentle stroke.

"You silly cat, you shouldn't touch one of those guys if they can sting you."

"He thought it would be even slower than he is," the sister said. "He thought he could beat it and got carried away."

Hachi dropped his brow at these unkind words, and Tsutomu grimaced.

"Don't say that! He tried to kill it because he knows you all hate caterpillars. I'm sure of it."

"Sorry," the sister said, chastened. Later, she gave Hachi a snack.

The pads on his paw continued to sting, but not so badly that he had to be taken to the vet.

Caterpillar season was drawing to a close when the phone rang one evening.

The uncle answered. He'd just finished taking a bath.

"Hey, it's been so long! How have you been? I see. And Noriko-chan's well, too?"

The uncle happily chatted on, decked out in just his underpants and oblivious to the horrified look the aunt shot at him.

"Oh, that sounds fine. Please, come over. Hachi would love to see you."

The uncle hung up, and the aunt asked, "Who was that?"

"It was Satoru-kun. You remember—he sends us a New Year's card every year."

Hachi's ears pricked up. That name shot through him like an electric current.

Satoru.

"Oh, the boy who lives with Noriko-chan . . ."

"Right, right. That's the one."

"He's the boy who first had Hachi," Tsutomu said. "He's the same age as me, I think?"

"Really? He said he's going to work part-time in the summer and come to see Hachi."

"Where does he live now? His aunt was always being transferred for work, wasn't she?"

"He said they're in Yamanashi now."

"Wow, so he's working to earn money just to come to see Hachi! The guy must really love cats."

Satoru. Satoru. Satoru.

"In his New Year's card every year he always asks us to say hello to Hachi. He must have really loved him."

"If that's the case, he should have had his aunt bring him here sooner."

"Noriko-chan's so busy, though. And since she took him in and all, I don't think he felt he could ask her to."

*H*achi, take care!
He'd smiled through his tears, waving and waving.

W hen Satoru comes over, you be nice to him, Tsutomu."
"Well, I'll treat him like anyone else. But—he loved Hachi so much, so I guess he must be a pretty good guy."

T he first person to call him *laid-back* wasn't Tsutomu.
Hachi's memory rewound clearly to the moment when Tsutomu and Satoru had overlapped.

Satoru must surely have grown like Tsutomu, healthy and tall.

༙

S o Satoru was coming to visit this summer.

When would the summer holidays begin? The days were growing steadily longer, the shadows steadily deeper.

This was the season when Tsutomu's face became the darkest.

Every day was so hot now, the holidays should begin soon, right?

I hope he comes soon, Hachi thought. *When Satoru and Tsutomu meet, I'm sure they'll get along.*

Hachi had waited so long, he couldn't wait any longer.

Maybe he got lost on his way over, Hachi thought, deciding to take a little look around the neighborhood. It was evening, when the heat of the sun was finally letting up.

He'd never been outside in the garden and decided not to overdo it. He'd start with one circuit around the building, and then gradually get a little further each time.

"Hachi seems to be going for walks these days," reported the aunt at dinner.

Tsutomu frowned.

"I just hope he doesn't get lost."

Not to worry, Hachi thought proudly. *I'm pushing the boundaries of my walks, one step at a time.*

"Just in case, let's put a collar on him, an ID tag," proposed the sister, buying one the very next day.

"He might hate it."

Hesitantly, the sister attached the collar around Hachi's neck. He knew in an instant he could wriggle out of it if he made the effort, but he figured it would be too much trouble and so left it on.

"Well, he's always been the type of cat who goes with the flow," the second-eldest brother said, laughing.

Hachi had now got used to strolling around outside and, thinking that Satoru might still have trouble finding them, decided to expand the scope of his walks even further.

There was a big road he had never crossed. So many people seemed to cross over that road in his direction. When Satoru arrived, he would surely use this road, too.

Observing for a while how things were done, Hachi understood that if humans timed it right, they could cross safely on the striped part of the road without being in danger from any cars.

He tried it himself a few times and crossed safely over.

One day he was waiting for someone to cross over with when a young man suddenly sprinted across the striped section. Thinking he could make it, too, Hachi darted after him. Just then, a car blared its horn.

The young man had made a dash, but Hachi froze on the spot.

With a huge *bang*, Hachi was sent flying. When he realized what had happened, he began to spit up blood. The pain in his chest was so intense, he couldn't cope.

"My God, it's a cat!" screamed a woman.

"Hachi!"

In a flash, someone ran over and scooped him up.

Was he not able to see the dark face because his eyes were blurry, or was it because it was backlit by the setting sun? *Gosh*, he thought, *I can't tell if this is Satoru or Tsutomu.*

But either one is okay, he decided.

⤳

Satoru figured he could find their place by just asking for directions as he went, but his relatives had said they'd come to meet him at the station, at the exit for the Shinkansen train. Satoru exited where they were supposed to meet and a tanned-looking boy—or would you say young man? he was at a kind of in-between age—called out to him.

"Hey, are you Satoru Miyawaki?"

"Yes, I am."

"Nice to meet you. I'm Tsutomu."

Tsutomu turned out to be the same age as Satoru, which made Satoru realize—a little late, perhaps—that he, too, was at the same indeterminate age.

"I'm so sorry you came all this way and—this happened."

"It's okay. None of you are to blame."

They had already told him that the very day before Satoru was due to arrive, Hachi had passed away after being hit by a car.

Tsutomu led Satoru home, where the uncle and aunt gave him a warmhearted welcome. "We're happy to see you," they said. "But we're so sorry this happened."

The same words that Tsutomu had used, and this made Satoru smile.

"And after I'd promised to make sure Hachi was happy," the uncle said.

"I'm sure he was happy, being raised with your family," Satoru replied.

In the living room, they had displayed a photo of Hachi, along with some offerings, at the family's little Buddhist altar, just as you would for a deceased relative. Dotted around were photos of previous cats.

To have lived with this family, Hachi must have been happy and contented until the very end of his life.

"And his grave is where—?"

"We couldn't afford anything fancy like a plot at a pet cemetery. Instead, we buried him in the mountains," the uncle replied. "Tsutomu said he'd take you there tomorrow."

Tsutomu nodded. "It's a half hour by train."

"Thank you."

That night the sister and eldest brother came home, and plates of delicious food were served for dinner, in a sort of celebratory feast.

They all shared stories about Hachi.

"He was kind of slow, which I thought was cute," the sister said.

"Don't ever say he was slow," Tsutomu snapped at her. "Hachi was a laid-back, gentle cat."

Satoru couldn't help but laugh.

"Exactly that. He was a laid-back, gentle cat."

The next morning, after breakfast, Satoru and Tsutomu set off for the grave.

They bounced around in the train along an old branch line, and after half an hour they were out in the countryside, among hills and valleys. The station where they got off was surrounded by fields.

For a while, they hiked along a farm track, Tsutomu leading the way toward the hills.

"It'd be a lot easier if we had come by car, but Dad has to work today," he explained.

As they climbed up the slope of a woodland path, they naturally fell into talking about Hachi. They'd already discussed their school and the clubs they were in, and Hachi was the only shared topic left.

"Once when a mouse appeared all of a sudden, Hachi was so shocked he fell backward on his behind," Satoru said.

"Really? Yeah, I can imagine that."

"Because he was so laid-back. Being hit by a car is also something I could see happening to him. He must have been so shocked when he saw it coming."

"No, that's not how it was." Tsutomu's face screwed up in regret. "I got there right after he was hit. I was just passing by after baseball practice on my way home. A woman who saw it all told me. Hachi was following a man who had crossed against the traffic signal. Hachi was smart and cautious and I'm sure he thought that, if he crossed with a human, he'd be safe."

Tsutomu was staring straight ahead, trying his best to hold back the tears.

"If that idiot hadn't done that, I'm sure Hachi wouldn't have tried to cross. If I find that guy, I'm going to beat him to a pulp."

"If you find him, let me know, too."

Tsutomu shot him a look of surprise. "You don't look like you'd be tough in a fight."

"You're right. So I'll wait until you've beaten him up, Tsutomu-kun, and then I'll give him a final punch."

"You're nuts." Tsutomu burst out laughing. He turned away quickly and wiped his eyes with his arm, pretending it was sweat.

At the top of the hill was a sunny, open field. Tsutomu led Satoru over to the furthest corner.

Dotted around were small granite blocks, one of which was brand-new.

"Dad got an endpiece from a friend of his who's a stone-mason. We couldn't afford to buy a plot in a real pet cemetery."

"This is perfect. It's so pleasant and sunny."

They scattered crunchy cat food in front of Hachi's grave and opened packets of cooked chicken breast and cheese, which they placed carefully around. They'd brought along extra cat food and offered it at the graves of their other cats, all of whom were buried there.

"My parents died in a car accident, too."

"Yeah," Tsutomu murmured. He seemed to know already.

"When I got back from a school trip, they were gone."

"Yeah," Tsutomu said, nodding again.

"The souvenir I'd bought for my dad was a good-luck amulet to prevent car accidents."

Tsutomu could no longer simply nod, and hung his head in silence.

"This one."

Satoru pulled an amulet out of his bag. It was a key ring with a good-luck *maneki-neko* figure attached, the kind with one paw raised, beckoning you.

"Have you kept it all this time?"

"The one I brought back originally is in his coffin, which got burned when he was cremated. Before I got here, I stopped off in Kyoto, where we'd been for our school trip, and looked for another one. I don't know if it's exactly the same, but it looks like it."

The key ring was the kind you could find anywhere. A childish-looking thing, the type kids would choose. These trinkets never changed, even over time.

"That *maneki-neko* looks like Hachi," Tsutomu murmured as he rolled the amulet in his fingers. Satoru knew he would notice the resemblance right away. Because Tsutomu was the boy who called Hachi a laid-back, gentle cat.

"That's why I bought it. Though it wasn't in time to give to Dad."

At the time, so many thoughts had raced through his mind.

He'd been angry at himself for buying an amulet that didn't get there in time. *What an idiot I was.*

Another thought: maybe it was because he'd bought this cheap little amulet that his mom and dad had been in that accident.

"But when I heard about Hachi's accident . . ." He firmly pushed down the lump rising in his throat. "I thought maybe I should have given the amulet to Hachi."

Too late now. He was fully aware of it.

But he had intended to give the amulet to Hachi. He knew Tsutomu would understand why. Hachi was a laid-back, gentle cat, after all.

"Could you keep it, Tsutomu-kun?"

Tsutomu blinked in surprise.

"I'm sure Hachi will be happy if you take it."

He hadn't arrived in time for his father. Or for Hachi.

If Tsutomu could take it, though, it would be in time, finally.

"All right."

Tsutomu slipped the amulet into his back pocket.

"We should be heading back. If we miss the return train, we'll have to wait a long time."

Satoru put his hands together in front of Hachi's grave.

"I'm counting on you, Hachi."

As they made their way back across the field, he thought he heard a cat meowing. He looked over at Tsutomu.

"Might be Hachi," Tsutomu murmured.

"Might be," Satoru replied.

They sauntered back down the mountain path, and their laughter continued to ring out as they went.

Life Is Not Always Kind

Allow me to introduce myself. I am a cat. The name is Nana—

That's me trying to imitate the greatest-ever cat in Japan, the one in Natsume Soseki's famous book *I Am a Cat*. But introducing myself like this is a bit lame, because that cat didn't have a name, whereas I do. And it would have to be a fairly elderly cat to say something like, *Allow me to introduce myself.* I'm still a young cat, after all, so let me put a lid on any nostalgia right here and right now.

I am, by the way, an upstanding male cat, but with the girlish name of Nana, if you can believe it. I had nothing to do with it.

Satoru, my owner, gave me the name without asking me. He's a good guy, though sometimes a bit oblivious. The name came from my cute, hooked tail. The reason he gave me this name is a bit absurd—my hooked tail from above looks like the number seven, *nana* in Japanese.

Satoru might lack good sense when it comes to names, but as a human he's the perfect roommate. And I'm the perfect cat for a human's roommate.

We've been sharing a pleasant life together for five years now, but something came up recently that cast a shadow across it.

Unavoidable circumstances meant Satoru could no longer look after me. Once he found out this was the case, he wasted no time in sorting it out. He used all his contacts to find someone new to take care of me. As soon as anyone showed willing, he took me around to see them, as if he was matchmaking, setting up a *miai*, or formal marriage interview.

Honestly, he didn't need to go to the trouble. Satoru adopted me when I was already a grown-up cat. In other words, until that moment, I had been living the life of a full-fledged alley cat. Even though I settled down quickly as a house cat, I still had a touch of the feral in me.

If I couldn't live with Satoru anymore, then all I had to do was go back to my previous life. But Satoru had already shrugged off his own worries to find me a new home, though in doing so, he had totally underestimated me, in all honesty.

So Satoru began taking me around to see all these people he seemed to know. Naturally, I had no intention of letting any of these *miai* succeed. So far we've had three such meetings, and I made sure every single one of them fell through.

In our travels, we've always taken the silver van. When it's a long trip, we bring along a cat toilet, and all the facilities are top-notch as far as a cat is concerned.

I was hoping he'd give up on all these meetings, but driving around in the silver van wasn't so bad, so I went along without any complaints.

The upshot is I've glimpsed way more of the world than your average cat. I've seen two towns where Satoru grew up when he was a child, one farming village, some rice fields, the ocean and Mount Fuji. I grew up in the city, so ordinarily I should go my whole life without seeing anything beyond my day-to-day surroundings.

But I've now seen more of the world than any other cat in Japan. And for the rest of my life I'll never forget the experiences Satoru and I have shared.

And now we were off on our fourth journey together.

The silver van was heading west. We drove out of Tokyo in the late afternoon, chasing after the evening sun as it set in the sky. Behind the wheel, Satoru's face glowed orange in the light. Even with the visor lowered, it was too bright for him, and he blinked over and over.

He glanced over at me, curled up in the passenger seat, and laughed.

"Your pupils are like the thinnest of threads, Nana."

Cats' eyes have amazing pupils. Depending on the brightness, they can adjust the amount of light that gets in. In bright light our pupils become really narrow, and then grow big and round when it's dark.

My pupils right now would be vertically as thin as they could be.

"There's a saying that a man's eyes should be narrow and straight, while a woman's should be round as a ball, but your eyes are pretty adaptable, Nana, since your pupils can go thin like that if need be."

I suppose you're right, I thought, twitching my whiskers. Satoru's eyes weren't adaptable at all, since even when it was bright, his pupils didn't grow thin like mine. At times like this, I wished I could trade eyeballs with him. Because all I have to do when it's too bright is curl up in the passenger seat and sleep.

"Oh, we're almost in Kyoto," murmured Satoru as he glanced up, apparently reading the road signs as they flashed by.

"If we took the Shinkansen train, it'd only take about thirty minutes to get all the way to Kobe."

Satoru was looking a bit tired, what with heading into the sunset for so long.

"Why don't we take a break in Otsu?"

Fine by me. I could do with a snack.

First, though, I thought I'd take a toilet break, and was about to slip through onto the backseat where the cat toilet was.

In the glow of the setting sun, a huge body of water suddenly appeared up ahead.

What the—? With my paws on the dashboard and my hind legs on the seat, I craned my neck forward.

"Caught your attention, did it?" Satoru laughed. "Isn't it amazing? It's the biggest lake in all Japan."

Isn't this the ocean? You're saying this huge body of water isn't the ocean?

"Let's stop by and check it out."

No, thanks, I'm good. The ocean from afar looked pretty, and there were all those fish swimming around—yum—and it was all very romantic, but when we got closer there was the frightening roar of those giant waves. Like in a horror film or something.

"Actually, if we stop here, we'll be late in getting to the other side."

Yes, indeed, best not to overdo things.

So Satoru stopped at a rest area for a break until the setting sun wasn't so bright anymore. He gave the lake a miss, and we continued on our way.

Dinner for me that evening had been a simple healthy cat tuna blend, but Satoru sprinkled some katsuobushi flakes on top and I ended up eating way too much and feeling stuffed.

It's a physical fact that animals become sleepy when they've eaten a lot.

I curled up on the passenger seat, and after that I don't remember a thing. Only that at some point Satoru was stroking my back like he was at a loose end, and I thought drowsily that he must have hit a traffic jam.

I woke to the sound of the engine groaning to a halt, and when I lifted up my head, I saw Satoru unbuckling his seat belt. Had we arrived at our hotel?

"Are you awake? I took a little detour before we got to the hotel."

Satoru reached out his arms and, after I'd arched my back to get the kinks out, he scooped me up. As I got out of the car, the cool night air tickled my nose and I let out a sneeze.

The sun was long gone, the mountain ridges etched in deep shadows that seemed to suck up the darkness.

"See?"

Resting in his arms, I turned around in the direction he indicated. *Whoa!*

At the foot of the hills below us was a sea of sparkling lights. As if it was still daytime in that single spot.

Amazing. Humans could make night into day.

"They call this a million-dollar view."

So they used a currency to express this, something that was keyed to a human value system alone. And a foreigner's currency, to boot. I let out a big yawn.

"Okay, so a million dollars at today's exchange rate would be, what? About 800 million yen?"

Satoru went through some mental arithmetic until he figured it out.

"That would come to about 4.8 million cans of soft, savory chicken cat food."

Now *that* was something. I studied his face again. I could eat, what?—a packet a day—and still not finish before I died.

Hmm—a night view worth 4.8 million cans of tasty

chicken breast meat. I looked down again on the sea of lights with fresh eyes.

Still—given a choice between the view and 4.8 million cans of tasty meat?

I'd take the cans, any day.

"What? You're tired of it already?"

Well, lights were just . . . lights, I thought, and once again let out a huge yawn.

Our hotel advertised itself as the only place in the area that was pet friendly, allowing animals to stay in the same room. Sure enough, when we checked in I caught a whiff of all the dogs and cats that had passed through.

We'd both eaten dinner at the rest area earlier, so all that was needed was to get ready for bed and go to sleep.

The room was on the smallish side but clean, and comfortable enough, though I deducted points for the fact that the TV wasn't one of those boxy-shaped ones I preferred.

The B&B we had stayed at before, run by Satoru's friends, was, by those standards, much better. You could look all over Japan, but hotels and suchlike offering boxy TVs for cats to sleep on were few and far between. We weren't allowed to walk down the common hallway here, but the fact that it allowed people to stay with their cats made this one of the better hotels, in my book.

As I was slinking around the room, inspecting it, Satoru

took a bath. From behind the closed door, I could hear him humming 20 percent louder than usual, so I knew he'd filled up the tub and was having a nice leisurely soak.

He finally emerged from the bathroom, and I slid by him to have a look for myself. After running a bath, there had to be some water still left in the tap.

I'm not sure why, but for some reason the water left inside a turned-off tap always tastes better than the water in my bowl. After Satoru finishes his bath, I always drink the water from the tap.

So at that point I simply followed my usual habit. I had no idea what a terrible miscalculation this would turn out to be.

"Nana! You can't drink that water!" screamed Satoru.

It's a universal given that a cat can drink whatever water he likes, in whatever way he prefers, so I ignored Satoru as he tried to stop me, and took a flying jump up onto the bath. I had figured the tub had a cover over it to keep the water hot, the way it usually does.

Not this one.

For a split second I had time to screech before I took an unexpected dive into the hot bubbly water. It had been draining out and the bath was only half full, but that was enough for me to get completely soaked.

"Hotel baths don't have covers like at home!"

You should have told me that!

I tried to scramble up onto the edge of the tub, but was so drenched I couldn't keep my footing. The bath was too slippery for my claws to get a foothold, and boosting myself up solely on leg power was, naturally, beyond me.

As I splashed about in the hot water, Satoru ran in and scooped me up.

He put me down on the floor and I gave myself a big shake, trying to get as much of the water off my wet, matted fur as I could. I dashed out of the bathroom and was about to settle down to groom myself when Satoru strode quickly over again.

"Don't do that, Nana! The water's still soapy!"

He picked me up and took me back to the bathroom.

Don't do that? Okay, but what about my soaked torso? Holding me tightly below my belly, Satoru closed the bathroom door behind him with his foot.

"This is a good chance to give you a shampoo—I'll just use a little soap."

Help!!!!!!!!!!!

I scrambled free of him, but the door to the bathroom was closed, like a wall before me. I scratched and scratched, but it did not budge open even a crack.

"There's no running away!"

Satoru lathered up the soap and pinned me down firmly with his big hands. Then he lifted me back into the now-drained bathtub and began to scrub me.

Aaaaargh!

Satoru ended up having to get fresh pajamas and towels from the hotel. Water had been splashed all over the tiny bathroom.

I was resting on a towel, doing my best to groom myself, when Satoru brought over a hair dryer. I furrowed my brow in a fierce glare and wrinkled my nose.

If you aim that rackety thing at me, there will be a split in our relationship that won't be restored by tomorrow. Are you willing to risk that?

"You'll catch a cold," Satoru tried to explain weakly, but he seemed to pick up on my vibes and meekly put the dryer away.

Satoru's mobile phone started to play a lighthearted melody. The kind of tune where you expect a dove to fly out.

"Hello . . . Yes, we just got here a little while ago! Thank you so much for checking."

I gathered this was the person we'd be meeting tomorrow. Satoru's professor from when he was in college, who was now working in a nearby part of Japan.

"All right, then we'll see you after one o'clock tomorrow!"

After hanging up, Satoru turned to me.

"If things work out, then tomorrow I guess we'll be saying goodbye . . . I shouldn't have made you so mad."

Not to worry. I'd make sure to bust it all apart tomorrow.

I'd pretty much dried myself off and my tongue was getting tired, so I took possession of the single-seat sofa and curled up.

I woke up in the middle of the night feeling chilly, since my fur was still a little dampish.

Nothing I could do about it, I thought, figuring all I could do was pout until the next morning.

I stepped off the armchair and headed to Satoru's bed.

Leaping up to his pillow, I sniffed around the edge of the futon cover. Satoru lifted the cover up to make space for me to crawl under. I'd trained him well.

I snuggled through toward his feet, turned around and shuffled back up to his pillow and lay down. Satoru, still prone, scratched the top of my head.

He was mumbling something, and when I looked over, I realized it was my name. And in the darkness I could see his eyes were gleaming with tears.

Good grief. If he was going to cry about it, then why let me go? Humans were always so chock-full of contradictions.

How nice it would be if humans, like us animals, were multilingual. Then I could explain why he didn't have to go to the trouble of finding a new owner for me. I'd tell him that, as an unabashed former alley cat, I would simply go back to being a proud stray.

I stretched my neck forward and licked around Satoru's eyes. My tongue tasted a slight saltiness.

"Nana, that hurts," Satoru said, pressing his fingers on my whiskers to push me away.

Now what kind of response was that?

༈

Satoru Miyawaki was in a bit of a bind and had to give his cat away and was urgently looking for someone to adopt him. This news had reached a couple of friends who had attended a seminar on regional industrial development with Satoru at a Tokyo university ten years earlier.

The couple—students at the seminar who had later got married but who now ran a B&B in Kofu—had made an attempt to adopt Satoru's cat, but their own dog had not approved and they couldn't cope with both.

The couple had since been in touch with Hisashi Kubota, an assistant professor in the economics department at the time of the seminar. The wife had remembered that the professor was fond of animals.

Satoru Miyawaki still hadn't found anyone to take the cat from him, they explained to Kubota, so if he felt able to, could he consider doing so himself?

The professor was living in a condo with his dog, Lily, who had been brought up alongside an elderly cat and had grown fond of it. Whenever he spotted a cat on one of their walks, he'd wander over, only to be harshly rebuffed, leaving him discouraged.

After the old cat passed away and there was no longer a cat around at home, Kubota thought that if he could find a cat to replace it, Lily might stop chasing cats outside and getting his nose scratched.

Would Satoru Miyawaki be willing to entrust his beloved cat to him? Concerned that he might not, Kubota didn't contact him directly but replied to the couple who'd first been in touch.

"Please tell Miyawaki that if he'll allow me to adopt his cat, then I'm ready," he told them.

A reply came back not from the couple but from Satoru himself, and by phone.

"Professor, it's been ages!"

From the sound of his cheerful, friendly voice, he hadn't changed at all, even though Kubota felt sure they hadn't parted on very good terms all those years ago, that there had been some ill feeling about something. Had he sent him off with a smile on graduation day? Kubota thought that he must have done.

"Since we'd parted on such awkward terms," Satoru said, "I definitely wanted to see you again."

Ahhh. So there really had been some ill feeling, Kubota realized, as he was immediately yanked back to reality.

"I'm thrilled, of course, that you'd consider taking in Nana for me," Satoru said, "but I'm happier still about having this opportunity to see you again."

He did seem genuinely happy. That made Kubota happy, but a bit ashamed, too. This guy was more than twenty years younger than him, he thought, and yet so much more generous and mature.

"Right. Well, when I hear that one of my former students needs help, I can't very well ignore him, now, can I? I love animals, and my dog loves cats, too."

Kubota tried to sound as kindly as he could.

They checked their calendars to arrange a date, but Kubota's weekends were full, and since Satoru said a weekday was fine, Kubota looked at his teaching schedule and found an opening in the middle of the week.

"How will you get here? If you're taking the Shinkansen train, shall I pick you up at the station?"

But Satoru said he'd be driving.

"You wouldn't expect it of a cat, but Nana loves to go for drives," he said. "If you do take him in, Professor, please take him out for a drive every once in a while."

"I often go to the dog park, so I could take Nana along," Kubota suggested.

After their casual chat, they hung up, and now the day had arrived when Satoru would actually be coming to his apartment.

The previous evening after coming home from his teaching, Kubota had done some cleaning, hauling out the vacuum cleaner sooner in the week than he normally would. After vacuuming, he noticed the dust on the furniture and brought out the feather duster. For the first time in a long while, he remembered how his wife would scold him: *Use the duster* before *you vacuum!*

Cut me some slack here, he thought. Wanting to dust in the first place proved how motivated he was to clean, didn't it?

He planned to have tea and cakes waiting, but wondered if Satoru would have eaten lunch already. One o'clock was an awkward time. Maybe he should have invited him for lunch?

He'd ask him when he got there, and if he hadn't eaten, then maybe he could have some sushi delivered? Which meant he'd have to restrict himself to a small lunch to leave room for the sushi.

After his morning classes had finished, Kubota stopped by the student cafeteria and, after much deliberation, decided to go with the tempura udon. But this didn't seem enough, so he added a three-pack of Inarizushi to his order. Maybe I shouldn't have added the rice balls, he thought, gazing at his protruding stomach, but if Satoru has already eaten lunch and they didn't get to have the sushi, this would turn out to be light fare.

Thinking it would be best for Lily and Nana to meet after Nana had had a moment to get used to his new surroundings, he put Lily in his cage in a back room.

The front doorbell chimed. He answered the intercom and the same voice he'd heard on the phone announced: "Hello, it's me, Satoru Miyawaki."

He opened the door and there was Satoru standing on the mat, cat carrier in hand. His lanky build hadn't changed since his student days. And neither had his winning smile.

"Welcome. Come on in."

Kubota was thinking his voice sounded a bit shrill. Satoru looked at him, eyes widening. "My goodness, Professor. You've grown so plump!"

Caught off guard, Kubota burst out laughing. That's right—that's the kind of student he was. Friendly, but with a mouth on him, too. This had often had the other seminar students in stitches.

"Somehow I've managed to put on twenty kilos in the last ten years."

"That's not good at all. You'd better go on a diet."

"It's too much trouble to cook for myself, so I end up eating out all the time," Kubota said as he showed Satoru into the living room.

"Wow, your place is neat as a pin! Hard to believe you live all by yourself here."

"Well, so far, so good. I've been a widower for so long." He didn't breathe a word about all the cleaning he'd done the day before.

"And your children?"

"Both went to school in Tokyo."

"So they're that grown-up now. How old are they?"

"My son just graduated from university, and my daughter has just started."

As he placed Nana's carrier on the floor, Satoru sighed. "I used to think there was such a big age gap between a college student and an elementary school pupil, but now that I'm out and working, the gap doesn't seem that great anymore."

The year Satoru had graduated, Kubota's son would have been in his last year of elementary school.

"It wouldn't be so strange if he and I ended up working together. My company hired new college graduates this year."

The thought occurred to Kubota that it wouldn't be odd,

either, if he had a son Satoru's age. If he'd got married earlier, that is.

And this made him realize what a childish attack he'd made on Satoru back when he was the same age his son was now.

Satoru opened the carrier and peered inside. But Nana showed no sign of emerging.

"Sorry, but he never wants to come out right away," Satoru apologized. "Hey, Nana," he said.

"That's okay. Let him be as cautious as he wants. It's a sign of intelligence," Kubota said, touching his arm to stop him pulling Nana out.

Satoru smiled, seemingly happy to hear his cat being praised.

"Have you had lunch?" Kubota asked.

"I did. I figured you would grab a bite at college."

"Come to think of it, are there any restaurants that allow you to bring a cat in?"

"I left Nana back at the hotel and went out by myself before driving over here."

He explained that he'd parked in the spot suggested by Kubota.

"Sorry we don't have a spot for guests in front of our building."

Whenever anyone parked in front of the condo, the driver would be alerted because whoever parked there would get a ticket.

"Well, why don't you sit down. I'll make some tea. I'm sure Nana will choose to emerge at some stage."

As a teatime snack Kubota had bought some *imagawayaki* sweets on the way back from the campus. As soon as Satoru saw them, he broke into a smile. "So they still have these!" he exclaimed. "I haven't had them in such a long time. I don't know why, but having *imagawayaki* or those fish-shaped *taiyaki* cakes as a snack really makes me happy."

"In this part of Japan they call them *kaitenyaki*," Kubota said, displaying some trivia he'd picked up after moving there.

Satoru looked genuinely surprised. "Is that right?" he said.

Kubota smiled at his interest. As a student, Satoru had always struck him as someone who listened carefully. He had also been a bit of a disrupter who clowned around and made people laugh, but he always took his studies seriously. Which is why Kubota had given him special attention. He'd liked him so much that, at times, he worried that he was favoring him over the other students.

So why hadn't he realized it at the time? That when such a sensitive student as Satoru was refusing to back down, there must have been a very good reason for it.

If he could rewind time, he wished even now he had bitten his lip and not said anything.

༄

The first time Kubota was aware of this student named Satoru Miyawaki was at a series of introductory lectures he was giving on the local economy.

In one of his classes, he happened to mention a book about a village that had once been successful in raising the profile of local industry, a book that was particularly relevant to the subject they were discussing.

Some time later, a student had come up to him.

"I really enjoyed the book that you mentioned in your class the other day," he said.

He hadn't brought it up as assigned reading or anything, and frankly Kubota himself had forgotten he'd even mentioned it.

"So you went to the trouble of reading it, did you?"

"Yes, they had a copy in the university library."

Kubota's first thoughts were skeptical, that this was someone who had possibly missed a lot of classes and was trying to earn extra points, but the student had then launched into a lengthy monologue about the book, which he had clearly enjoyed reading.

"It seemed less like a straight factual account than a kind of adventure story. Like turning adversity into a positive way forward, and it reminded me a bit of an RPG."

"RPG? Meaning?"

"Ah—that's right. People your age don't play video games much, do they? I'm talking about role-playing games—*Dragon Quest*, *Final Fantasy*, things like that."

Ah, Kubota thought, *I get it now.*

"The ones my kids are always pestering me to buy for them."

"Right, right—that's what I mean."

The way he described his response to the book was so typical of young people, and Kubota found it refreshing.

"You finish one mission and then another begins. And you build up experience points every time. I haven't read much nonfiction, but I was amazed by how dramatic the book was."

"Truth can be stranger than fiction, like they say. Documentaries about successful projects are especially compelling. They can make you feel hopeful. When ambitious people get together, the future can seem full of opportunity."

The bell rang, signaling the end of break.

"I'm sorry, I've taken up all your time."

The student was walking away when Kubota stopped him.

"What is your name and what are you studying?" he asked.

"My name's Satoru Miyawaki. I'm a second-year student in economics."

If Kubota hadn't asked him, Satoru might well have walked away without ever introducing himself. He'd just wanted to share his thoughts on a book with someone else who'd enjoyed it, it seemed.

From then on, Kubota would occasionally lend Satoru books from his own personal library.

"There are lots of great books in the seminar room as well, so feel free to borrow those, too."

Another professor was nominally in charge of the seminar, but he was such a well-known economist, busy with external TV appearances and speaking engagements, that he was rarely on campus. So Kubota was, in reality, leading the seminar, and had taken over most of the bookshelves in the seminar room.

It would be great if this student were in his seminar, Kubota thought, and the following year his wish came true.

Satoru applied for Kubota's seminar with two friends, a boy and girl, to whom Satoru had recommended it. The young woman's family ran a fruit orchard in Yamanashi, as Satoru happily explained to Kubota: "When I suggested that she apply, I told her the seminar would be helpful in running their family business." The other friend, the young man, seemed to be a tagalong, going wherever the girl went. That happened all the time with young people.

Kubota's seminar focused on fieldwork, and very soon it was Satoru who proposed a theme for their summer training camp.

"Miss Sakita said her family's happy for us to use their place as a practice location," he announced. Sakita was the girl whose family ran the fruit orchard.

She and Satoru, and their fellow student Sugi, turned out to be friends from high school.

The fieldwork that Satoru proposed was to divide the seminar students into two teams who would compete with each other to see who could sell the most fruit from a roadside stand. In exchange for helping with farmwork in the orchard, Sakita's family had said they'd be willing to finance the project by providing the produce. This way, they also got free labor during their busy season.

The orchard had already set up roadside stands at several

locations, and on the days of the students' competition, they let them take over the stands.

With two competing teams, it was unclear how they should divide up the students.

Seniors versus the juniors was one idea, but then the juniors, with the orchard owner's daughter plus the two boys who'd already worked there, would have an advantage, wouldn't they? But that said, the seniors had a year more field-work experience, right? Okay, but what about grades? If one team didn't sell as much, would that affect their grades?

Kubota told them clearly that their grades would be based solely on the reports they turned in. Finally the details of the proposed competition were settled.

"Sir, even if our grades are based on our written work, if you give the winning team some sort of prize, that'd be a great motivator." This from one of the bratty seniors.

"Okay, what do you suggest? We don't want it all to get too serious."

"We're not kids. If we lose, we'll simply accept it."

"In that case—" It was Satoru who raised his hand. "How about giving the winning team premium pilsner beer when we make the toast?"

Pilsner was not in the all-you-can-drink promotion at the local izakaya and was an aspirational beer well out of reach of the students. But it wouldn't be too expensive for their supervisor to treat them to it. Satoru had been very tactful when it came to coming up with a compromise.

"Yeah, that'd be great," the students agreed.

"It's agreed, then—the winning team will have premium pilsner." Kubota accepted the idea straightaway, since it would not be a strain on his pocket, and inwardly he was grateful to Satoru.

During the students' summer training camp, the orchard supplied peaches and grapes from its vineyard.

The senior and junior teams each came up with their own strategy.

The seniors would provide free samples to potential customers, while the juniors went with selling substandard produce, which they'd sell at a discount. Each team would put up signs for drawing in customers, limited to one sign per team.

The junior team, however, wasn't allowed to put "Bargain Prices" on their sign, which they'd been planning on. And everything else they came up with to allure their customers with low prices was similarly vetoed. The juniors were none too happy with this decision, but there was too much of an advantage in advertising sale items compared to regular products.

In the end, the senior team chose "Try Your Samples Here" for their sign, while the juniors wrote "B Grade Fruit" on theirs.

From morning until evening, they worked at their roadside stands, and in the end the junior team won the day. This wasn't due to the price difference, it turned out, but to the position of the stands and the visibility of the signs. Their target customers were drivers on the highway, and the phrase "Try Your Samples Here" was a little too long for people to take in as they drove past.

"B Grade Fruit," written in three simple characters in Japanese, was pithier. The phrase also raised customers' expectations since it gave them the idea of getting a bargain.

If these had been stands aimed at pedestrian traffic, it was decided, the results may very well have been different. For browsers on foot, the idea of free samples had a lot more appeal.

At any rate, the students gathered a wealth of material from the fieldwork to put in their reports.

That was the final day of their summer training camp, and the orchard staff prepared a delicious dinner for them.

"Sir, thank you for all the help you've given my daughter," the orchard owner said, pouring some locally made wine into Kubota's glass. Kubota had forgotten to tell him that he wasn't much of a drinker.

"A friend of mine who runs a winery gave it to me, especially for this evening."

This made it even harder for Kubota to turn it down. Besides, the wine was quite tasty, and before he knew it he had become somewhat tipsy.

When he was just about to topple over, Satoru was there to lead him away from the party.

"Sir, we've laid out a futon for you."

Their lodgings were in an annex near the orchard. Just as

they got in, Kubota's legs gave way and he collapsed onto the futon.

"Thank you," he said. "I was about to make a fool of myself."

"People who can drink a lot have trouble imagining that others can't hold their alcohol. I'm not much of a drinker, either, so I kept my eye on you, sir. What I tend to do to avoid being given too much to drink is to help out as a server, but you didn't have that option."

Kubota had noticed that Satoru had indeed been cheerfully scurrying around like a busy mouse. But he hadn't realized why.

"I don't need to drink to have a good time, and I just wish they'd let me be."

Satoru seemed the type for whom the party atmosphere was enough.

"Is Miss Sakita's father a heavy drinker?"

"He certainly is. Back in high school, his son and I often got smashed together."

"Wait just a second. You were still minors, right?"

"Let's not go there. Sakita's father's the one who urged us on, so best take that up with him, not me." Satoru looked a bit ruffled, as if trying to avoid a subject he'd rather not discuss. "The person who really ended up being a drinker because of Sakita's father was Sakita herself," he went on after a pause, and laughed. "That's why she was complaining throughout this whole fieldwork project. She complained to me that since we're staying at hers, she's been made to help out so much she hasn't been able to relax and have a drink."

"I see. Maybe I pushed her too hard," Kubota said. "But it did turn out to be a very meaningful session. Thanks to you, for proposing it." He paused. "I'm so happy you ended up joining our seminar," he added suddenly, the alcohol doing the talking.

"Well, I had been thinking of attending a different seminar." Satoru was such an affable student that other professors had had their eye on him as well. "But I decided pretty early on to join yours."

"How come?" Kubota asked.

"I enjoyed discussing books with you, and when I first visited the seminar room, I got a good feeling about it."

Kubota mulled this over. What could have made him think that way, he wondered.

"The thing is, sir, you have photos of your family on your desk, don't you? Photos of you with your cat and dog, too, which really struck me."

"So you're a cat lover?"

Satoru blinked in surprise, the remark seemingly spot-on.

"Because you mentioned cats first."

Satoru nodded.

"I like both, but if I could have a pet, it would be a cat. I had one when I was a child."

"What was it like?" Kubota asked, and Satoru was only too happy to answer.

"His name was Hachi. A sensible cat, very gentle. There

was a mark on his forehead shaped like the character for eight"—/\—"while his body was white and his tail was black and hooked."

"A hooked tail, eh? Cats like that bring good luck."

"Is that right?"

Satoru seemed unaware of the concept of lucky cats. Kubota couldn't recall where he'd heard about it.

"The idea is that the hooked tail snags good fortune and brings it to you."

"Is that so," Satoru murmured, as if heaving a sigh. His eyes seemed to melt into a smile. "So cats with hooked tails should definitely be content, right? With good fortune hanging down from their tails."

"Well, logically, I suppose so."

"Mmm," Satoru said, nodding, and his eyes looked shiny. "When I saw your photos, sir, it made me wish I had had my cat for longer."

Circumstances had forced him to give up his cat, he said, and ask some relatives to adopt him.

"In any case, he had a hooked tail, so I'm sure he was happy."

"I'm glad!"

They passed the time contentedly talking about cats. That night Kubota had a dream about cats. The cat Satoru had talked about made an appearance.

The next morning when he told Satoru about it, his eyes lit up. "Really?" he asked. "Did he seem happy?"

"Hmm. I only saw him from afar. He was lying in the sun so I can't really say."

"If he was lying in the sun, he was definitely happy."

But Satoru still looked a bit put out.

"Hachi's a little cruel, though, to appear in *your* dreams, sir, and not in *mine*."

Satoru seemed seriously ruffled by this, which Kubota found amusing.

∽

Well, he did, didn't he? He appeared in your dreams, Professor, but not in mine."

"I remember thinking it was funny how much that upset you."

As I listened to their conversation, I found it all pretty funny. *Yep, Satoru's the type who does get miffed at things like that, Professor.* But I don't think that's what Hachi intended. He wouldn't have liked it at all that Satoru didn't dream about him.

From where he was sitting on the sofa, with his legs crossed, the professor turned to look at me. His voice was a little muffled so I couldn't catch everything, and so while they were deep in conversation, I decided to step out of the carrier.

"He really does look exactly like Hachi. When I first saw him, I was so surprised. His tail hooks in the opposite direction, though. But if you look at it from above, it's shaped like the number seven."

A lucky-seven hooked tail, Professor. I pride myself that it snags more luck for me than Hachi's did.

"I see. So you were fated to meet Nana."

Good point, Professor. Keep up the preaching. Satoru, how can you even consider getting rid of me when fate, in the guise of a lucky-seven hooked tail, brought us together?

"Oh, yeah—I bought some cake, too. Would you like some?"

The professor stood up, but Satoru stopped him. "No, really, I'm fine."

"You don't eat enough. Young people need to fill up more."

No, exactly! It's true, Satoru's appetite has got smaller these days, but the amount of sweet things you've brought out is nuts.

Satoru was at a loss from the start, just with the *imagawayaki*.

"Are you sure? Word among the students at school is that the cakes from that store are really tasty . . ."

The professor looked so deflated that Satoru gave in. "Oh, okay, just one small piece, then."

When the professor left the room, I strolled toward Satoru and leaped up onto his lap.

"Ah, so you're out now, Nana. Does that mean you might like it here?"

Not at all—I just couldn't properly hear what you were saying. The professor has a dog somewhere, I gather, and if I pick a fight with him, that'll be more than a good enough reason for this plan to fall apart.

Watching the professor stroll back in and clatter around the kitchen, Satoru murmured, "Whatever happened between us when I was a student still seems to be bothering him."

I also thought he was acting a bit oddly.

He kept whipping out one sweet after another as if he wasn't sure what to do with himself. Any break in the conversation and the professor escaped to the kitchen, the outcome being this massive snack attack.

You didn't have to be a cat to understand what was going on. The man must have had some lingering sense of guilt toward Satoru.

"Here you go. Take as much as you like."

The professor had brought a box with six slices of cake. Way too many for just the two of them.

Satoru seemed to shudder, but exclaimed softly when he spied a thin slice of tangerine jelly. He seemed relieved to find something he might be able to stuff down.

"I'll have this one, thank you."

"That's one of their specials, available only this month."

The professor placed a large piece of rich Mont Blanc cake onto his own plate. He'd been gobbling one sweet after another and didn't seem to show any signs of stopping.

It was so funny to watch Satoru taking tiny bites of the jelly, by contrast, so he wouldn't finish it too quickly.

∽

Satoru and the Kubotas had always got along well, but things unfolded in Kubota's family that had soured their relationship.

His wife was found to have a malignant tumor. Satoru had just entered his senior year when the doctor told Kubota's wife she had only a year left to live.

At first Kubota didn't tell anyone, but when his wife was admitted to the hospital at the beginning of the autumn of that year, he could no longer keep it a secret. Kubota found himself running the house while looking after his two children and the pets and wasn't able to hide from his students the fact that he was paying frequent visits to the hospital as well. Even if all this hadn't been going on in the background, his seminar involved a lot of fieldwork, with a lot of close interaction with the students.

When he revealed what had been going on, the students took the initiative and rearranged the way the seminar was run to lighten the burden for the professor.

Satoru was the student who helped out most. He also took over a variety of domestic chores, food shopping and suchlike. And when Kubota couldn't arrange for a babysitter, Satoru would stay with the children at their home.

Satoru had a knack with children, and the kids grew fond of him. Until his wife went into the hospital, Kubota had asked his parents to look after their pets, but once Satoru had started coming over to the house every week, the kids announced they could take care of the animals themselves.

"Uncle Satoru," as they called him, seemed to enjoy looking after the pets so much that the kids wanted to copy him. Soon, the older boy was walking the dog. He'd go out with him after school, while it was still light outside.

"I'm sorry you have to go to all this trouble," Kubota said gratefully.

"Not a problem," Satoru said with a smile. "I look forward to seeing Mi-chan and John, too, and this year I only have one seminar left."

Impressively, he'd completed all his courses the previous year, and already had a postgraduate job lined up.

Satoru made it easy for people to lean on him, and that's exactly what Kubota did, updating him on his wife's condition and generally using him as a sounding board for worries.

Like a low-flying paper airplane in midflight, there was a lull in the severity of her condition, but then in the new year she went downhill quickly.

"I doubt she'll live to see the cherry blossoms," the doctor declared.

In the middle of it all, Satoru, who'd long since handed in his final thesis, came over to the seminar room unexpectedly. He was looking serious.

"What in the world is wrong?" Kubota asked. It would soon be visiting time at the hospital.

As if he'd made up his mind after coming to an important decision, Satoru said, "Sir, will you please tell your children about your wife?"

"What on earth are you talking about?"

Kubota had never told his children his wife had a terminal illness. His son was still only in sixth grade; his daughter was four years younger. He couldn't bring himself to confront them with the fact that their mother was dying.

Kubota was determined, till the very end, to take on the burden himself to keep the children from experiencing anything so bitter. The kids could find out when she was about to die, he had decided. He didn't want them to visit her, and to feel tormented by the inevitability of her death. He had always insisted that, until that unavoidable final moment, the children's contact with their mother would be a happy time for them.

"Stop meddling!" Kubota burst out.

"But, sir!"

The very thought of Satoru of all people intruding like this, and so late in the day! Kubota's anger surged all the more. He'd always thought Satoru had understood him best.

"Mind your own business!" he shouted.

But Satoru wasn't about to give up so easily.

"Sir, the kids already know!"

Kubota's blood began to boil.

"You haven't told them already, have you?"

"I haven't. But the kids sense it, that she doesn't have much time left."

If he'd listened to Satoru, he knew he would have understood his point. But by this stage he was jumping at anything.

He says he hasn't told them, but is that actually true? Even if he hasn't yet, there will come a time when he can't stay silent about it, thought Kubota.

"Just as your wife is important to you, that's how important their mother is to the kids! If their mother's going to die, the kids will want to say a proper goodbye! Please—let your children say goodbye to their mother!"

Satoru was making it sound as if Kubota didn't understand his kids' feelings, and that made him even more angry.

Satoru didn't even have children, so what was he talking about? It was as if he was saying he was the one who was closer to the kids.

"A parent should do what they need to do so their kids don't have any regrets!"

"You have no idea how a parent feels, so shut up!"

If only Kubota could rewind time and take back those words. How many times he had regretted it.

But Satoru continued to pick at his wound—he didn't back down a single step.

"I don't know how parents feel, but I know how *kids* feel! Because I am closer in age to your children, I understand how they feel more than you do!"

What feelings had wrung these words out of that young man that day?

"If they can make it in time, then kids, too, want to say goodbye! They'll want to tell her *I love you* and *Thank you!*"

Satoru's wailing voice rushed through his ears. He slammed down the shutter on the matter.

"Don't ever show your face here again! Don't you dare come

near my children! And there's no need for you to come back to the seminar, either!"

Despair was written all over Satoru's face.

This isn't any of his business, yet he looks so devastated.

Facing him, with this end-of-the-world expression, was frightening, and Kubota fairly ran out of the seminar room.

Until now, that was the last time they had seen each other.

It was true that Satoru didn't need to attend the seminar, because as previously stated, he'd already submitted his graduation thesis.

And it was an outstanding thesis.

Satoru went along with Kubota's demand and never came back. At first the other students wondered why he'd stopped coming, but Satoru glossed over his absence, telling them he had training to do for the job he had lined up.

Satoru's almost threatening insistence that he tell the children had stirred something up in Kubota, however. He mentioned it to Satoru's best friend, Sugi.

"He's so very worried about my children. Is there a particular reason why?"

Sugi seemed to understand. Maybe he'd heard something about it from Satoru.

"His parents died in a car accident when Satoru was a child. I heard it was when he was the same age as your son, sir. Maybe his feelings about it were so strong he couldn't help interfering . . ."

Please try to understand him. Sugi sounded as if he wanted to add this, if he could have done.

"I understand. Thank you," Kubota said, feeling utterly defeated.

The last time he'd been so stricken by someone's words was when he'd heard his wife's days were numbered.

The words he'd hurled at Satoru came back to haunt him.

You have no idea how a parent feels.

How did Satoru, who had lost both his parents when he was a child, feel when he heard this?

Because I am closer in age to your children, I understand how they feel more than you do.

Satoru understood all too well how children felt when they were suddenly told one day that their parents were dead.

Kubota wavered. Should he tell the kids, or not?

Then, when her final days were approaching, he told his son the truth.

"Mom doesn't have much longer to live."

His son began to weep, but he wasn't that shaken by the news. Maybe, as Satoru had said, he had a premonition of this already.

When they went to visit his wife in the hospital, most of the time she wasn't aware of her surroundings.

During the few moments when she was alert, his son repeated, over and over, *Thank you, Mom, I love you, Mom.* Then he more or less ordered his younger sister to do the same.

Kubota's wife could hardly speak, but the small nod she gave showed that she had heard.

If you can make it in time, you want to say *goodbye*. Want to say *thank you*, and *I love you*. The children had chosen the exact same words Satoru had used, so Kubota thought that maybe he *had* told them about his wife's condition after all, but when he heard his son repeat these for all he was worth, he felt it was okay even if Satoru had told them after all.

His wife died at the end of February, on a bitterly cold day.

After the funeral his son said, "Dad, thank you for telling me."

Kubota began to weep uncontrollably.

It was a burden lifted to know that he'd done the right thing. His daughter was still too young to understand what was going on, but he was relieved that his son hadn't had his chance to say a final goodbye snatched away from him.

About a month later, Satoru graduated.

Because he was still officially in mourning, Kubota wasn't at the thank-you party held for the teachers, but he did attend the graduation.

After the ceremony his seminar students came over to say hello. Unsure what to say to him since he was still in mourning, they kept it short.

Satoru was with them, but Kubota didn't speak. The situation made it fine not to do so.

Kubota had hurt Satoru, terribly, and he feared talking to him about it.

On his way out, Satoru bowed wordlessly to him.

Kubota acknowledged him with a nod.

᠕

Actually, I ended up telling my son that his mother didn't have long to live."

"Is that right?" Satoru responded to this confession with a small smile.

"If you hadn't told me to, I never would have let the children and their mother say a proper goodbye. But nevertheless . . ."

Kubota suddenly bowed his head.

"I am so, so sorry!"

"Please don't be, sir!"

In that moment, forgetting I was on his lap, Satoru rose to his feet. I mean, if it were any other cat, he would have tumbled to the floor, but I still clung on.

The professor raised his head, and Satoru looked relieved. He sat back down on the sofa.

"I'm to blame, too. I just vented because of what I went through myself as a child . . . But—you listened, and I'm thankful for that." Satoru bobbed his head. "I'm so sorry."

Kubota looked blank as he took in the unexpected apology.

"Recently I've been feeling like I finally understand how you and your wife must have felt. If, for instance, I were the one who had to say goodbye, I don't think I'd want my final hours to be sad. I would want to see my loved ones' smiles to the very end."

As a cat, I've noticed that people, young or old, always put themselves first: *This is the end, so I want to say goodbye, but until the very end I don't want to say a sad farewell.*

The boundary between adults and children is kind of vague. It's kids who believe in that boundary who announce that this is how adults should behave. Okay, so when do those kids become such mature adults?

"Still, it was as if I was preventing any other choice for you and your wife."

I'd say it's at the point where human beings let feelings and not instinct dictate how they should behave that they lose sight of the boundaries between adults and children that we animals have.

The only choice for humans is to flounder around, searching for a vague boundary, certain that they are right, and creatures like these only think they know what it means to be an adult.

At the time when Satoru thought he knew what a parent should do for his children, and by expressing these thoughts placed the professor in an awkward bind, he was behaving like a child. But another thing about humans is that it's when they are children that they can shake things up. With animals it's always the older ones who are the wisest.

"That's why I came here today. Not just to ask you to take care of Nana. I'm happy to be able to talk to you again, sir, and to be able to apologize."

Looking down, the professor shook his head. He was sniffling and seemed to be crying. He'd stopped rolling out the sweets in an attempt to cover up any silence.

He sat back and, looking Satoru in the eyes, began to reminisce. Then he began to laugh.

"There is no end to regrets, but it's time now. Time to bring my dog out to meet Nana." The professor stood up.

"What was his name again?"

"It's Lily. He loves cats, so not to worry."

The professor walked out of the living room, then came back, bringing the dog with him on a lead. In an instant, the dog had shaken off the professor and rushed into the room.

A CAT! It's a cat, a cat, a cat—let's play!

The creature that leaped at us, excitement ramped to the max, was a huge Great Dane.

Say what you will, but this guy was *way* too big.

So much so that Satoru stood up, ready to leave, and at the speed of light I clambered on top of his head. My back arched, my fur bristling, I did my best to threaten this Great Dane jumping for joy in front of us.

I mean, consider the size difference here. You think I can play with you when you're knocking us over?

With the Great Dane's front paws pushing at his waist, Satoru collapsed back on the sofa.

It's a cat!

Driven into a corner, I was in total crisis mode. Even if he didn't mean any harm, there was no way I could play with him when he was this worked up, and I got out of control, too, hissing and brandishing my claws at him.

Ow! the dog screamed.

Don't get any closer! Back OFF!

The Great Dane finally took a step back, but was still looking for his chance to play. *That hurt just now, you know! But anyway, when will you be in a better mood? When you're in a good mood, will you play with me?* He was obviously itching for action; his tail spoke a million words.

How was I supposed to be in a better mood in a situation like this, eh?

"Umm. Maybe Nana isn't so good with dogs?"

That's not the issue here, people—!

"No, I don't think that's the problem . . ."

Thanks for interpreting for me!

Because I was forced into threatening the monstrously huge Lily, it seemed I wouldn't end up going to the professor.

"Umm. It's too bad, but I don't think this is going to work for Nana," said Satoru.

"You think?"

The professor finally forced Lily into a back room in the apartment, getting pulled down himself in the process as Lily struggled to go back into the living room. But I digress.

"It's too bad about Nana's *miai*, but I'm so happy we could meet again."

"Me too."

No ill feeling left at all, teacher and pupil shook hands.

"Can I ask one question?" the professor asked, hesitantly, as they said goodbye.

"Of course, what is it?"

"Just before my wife died, my son said *thank you* and *I love you* over and over. The same words you said you would have spoken, if only you could have got there in time. Did you, perhaps, tell the children about my wife?"

"No, I did not," Satoru said, and smiled. "It's only natural he used the same words. Those are the only last words a child wants to say to a parent, if they are loved—*thank you* and *I love you.* Don't you think so?"

"I see," the professor said, understanding at last.

"You're the only one, Professor, who had the right to tell your children about their mother. That's why I quarreled with you so much."

"I see." The professor nodded several times, and smiled. "Thank you, for quarreling with me."

No, thank you, *Professor, for saying these words to Satoru.*

Satoru seemed choked up, so to say *thank you* on his behalf, I purred vigorously from inside my carrier.

After we left the professor's apartment, Satoru took a walk down the flagstone streets of the nearby town with its foreign look. We were sort of off the main road, so there weren't many cars about.

I was thinking of getting out of the carrier and stretching

my legs a bit myself. Lily had got his slobber all over me, and if I didn't do something about it, my carrier would stink of dog.

With my paws, I fiddled with the lock to the carrier and, seeing what I was up to, Satoru said, "Oh, Nana, do you want to come out?" and he unlatched it.

The white flagstones felt different on my pads from the asphalt streets I usually walked on. The stones were cool and pressing my pads against them felt good. Just walking on them made me feel healthier.

I heard the click of a camera and turned around to find Satoru training his mobile phone on me.

"It's like a painting, Nana." Satoru seemed to be checking his photo.

"Why don't we take the long way home."

As we walked, he took a few more photos of me. And I posed cutely to help him out.

By the time we arrived back at the parking lot and climbed into the silver van, the dog smell had been blown away by the wind.

Trying to push back on that vigorous, calf-sized dog had worn me out, and as soon as Satoru had driven off, I slipped into a deep sleep.

We're going to take a break, Nana."
Satoru's voice woke me gently, and I yawned and shook out my ears. Where were we? I stretched up to look out the window and saw a huge body of water right next to us.

"It's Lake Biwa. Remember I talked about stopping here on our way?"

But I told you we don't need to!

"Come on, let's get out."

Even if it wasn't like the horror movie of the sea, I still wasn't prepared to buy into it. But Satoru picked me up from my seat.

I braced myself for the heavy, gut-pounding crash of waves. But what I got was kind of anticlimactic.

On the lake there were just quiet little waves lapping on the shore, and no terrifying roar. The horizon looked the same, but the sea and a lake were totally different. *You know*, *taking a walk here wouldn't be so bad*, I thought, and wriggled out of Satoru's arms for a stroll along the shore.

There were other people strolling about, too, sightseeing at the lake like us.

An older man with a camera was wandering around. He looked over at Satoru, and when their eyes met, his expression brightened.

"Excuse me, but would you mind taking our picture?"

He seemed to want a photo of himself and his wife as a memento.

Satoru was often asked for a favor like this by passersby. Maybe because he seemed approachable.

"No trouble at all."

Satoru took the old-school camera from the man, and as he

looked through the finder, he called out to the couple, "Move just a smidge to your right, if you would. There you go. Perfect."

He snapped a photo of the elderly couple, smiling for all they were worth. "One more, just in case," Satoru said and clicked another photo.

"Thank you very much."

Thinking they were done, I sidled over to Satoru, and the old lady said, "Goodness. What have we here? Is this your cat?"

"He is. His name is Nana. Because his tail is hooked like the number seven."

The thought occurred to me each and every time: *Does he really have to explain my name to everyone he meets? Well—I suppose it makes him happy when people show an interest in me.*

"Is he traveling with you?"

"That's right."

The old lady clapped her hands, as if she had suddenly had some great idea.

"If you like, we can take a photo of the two of you together. We'll send it to you later."

"Oh, that's a great idea." The old man was into it, too.

"You don't mind?" Satoru clearly liked the idea as well.

He picked me up in a swoop and positioned himself where the lake could be seen in the background.

The old man took several photos and had Satoru check them.

"Are these okay?"

"Wow. Isn't this great, Nana? You look so cute in the photos."

Could he have made it any more obvious he was cat crazy? TMI, if you ask me.

Satoru gave the old couple his address and thanked them, and we left.

Not long after we got back to Tokyo, we received the photos.

To me the address written on the envelope looked like wriggling worms, but according to Satoru the handwriting was *superb*.

Included was a short note: "Thank you for the other day. I hope you're keeping well," it said, according to Satoru.

He scrutinized the three photos inside.

"These are the first-ever photos of us together, aren't they, Nana?"

Satoru lived alone, so we'd never taken any.

"I'm so happy," he said, and straightaway put them in a frame and displayed it in our flat.

We moved out of the apartment not long afterward, but in his next home, Satoru continued to display the photos. When the day came for Satoru to move into the hospital ward, which I wasn't allowed to enter, he took them with him there, too.

And when Satoru no longer needed the photos anymore, they found their way back to me.

I lived a happy life, looking at those photographs.

But that's another story.